THE FINAL TALES OF SHERLOCK HOLMES (VOLUME ONE)

By

Dr. John H. Watson, M. D.,

as edited by John A. Little

Paperback ISBN 978-1-78092-565-3
ePub ISBN 978-1-78092-566-0
PDF ISBN 978-1-78092-567-7

Published in the UK by MX Publishing
335 Princess Park Manor, Royal Drive, London, N11 3GX
www.mxpublishing.com

Cover design by www.staunch.com

Foreword.

No doubt the readers of this book will groan inwardly and mutter to themselves about yet another would-be writer pretending to be Watson and dreaming up more 'undiscovered' Holmes adventures in the hope of making a bob or two. While I have some sympathy with such a reaction, nothing could be further from the truth. For a start, I am not a writer, merely an editor. As you will soon discover.

The building known to all Holmes afficionados as 221B Baker Street had fallen into such disrepair by 1955 – thanks to the efforts of the German Luftwaffe, and many years after the detecting duo had passed on – that the local authorities deemed it unfit for habitation. It had to be knocked down. By my father, as it happens.

Eneder Little had built up a successful business as a builder in London, having been forced to emigrate from Ireland after the lunatic DeValera's disastrous economic policies of the 1930s. His company (Motto: 'No Job Too Big For Little') was granted the contract to demolish nos 220A, 220B, 221A, 221B, 222A, 222B, 223A and 223B Baker Street and rebuild a terrace of spanking new luxury four-bedroomed town houses, complete with all modern conveniences.

Before the buildings were due to be levelled, he was examining the basement at 221B when he discovered a tall dust-covered office cabinet hidden in a corner behind a dilapidated kitchen dresser. Having no keys, my curious father grabbed his jemmy and cracked open the lock that controlled the four metal drawers. There was nothing but wrapping paper inside the top one, but the other three drawers revealed a series of packages of

A4-sized spiral-back notebooks, each held together by two elastic bands in the shape of a cross. Never having read a book in his life apart from his annual accounts, he had no comprehension of his discovery. But he was a cautious man and decided to dump the lot into a cardboard box and take it home that night. And then promptly forgot all about them.

I became aware of this event only six months ago, when I was helping my mother and sister to clear out his effects the day after his funeral. He married late in life, and returned to live in Dublin towards the end of the 1970s with his wife and two small children.

I had climbed up a ladder into the attic and started handing down cartons of what was obviously rubbish – ancient account books from his building company, newspapers, magazines, old clothes, sporting equipment from his hockey and cricket-playing days – when I discovered a cardboard box, covered by some spare fibreglass insulation. Its bottom was lodged firmly between two beams and pulling it out almost caused my foot to slip off the beam and crash through the bathroom ceiling.

A rapid inventory produced sixteen packages, each of which contained a varying (one to nine) number of A4 notebooks, dated from 1925-1930. Later, when we were sitting down, exhausted after our day's work and with our shared grief, I asked my mother about them and she told me what little she could recall of their origin at 221B Baker Street. I pulled off the elastic band and opened the first notebook of a package marked February 1925, the earliest period. Intriguingly, it showed a faded red stamp with the tiny word 'Strand' repeated around the edges, and 'REJECT' in large letters diagonally across the middle. It was in surprisingly good condition, for a manuscript that had lain in its cardboard coffin for over eighty years.

I had only to finish a single chapter to realise what I held in my hand. All my life I had been a great fan of Holmes and Watson, and had read their exploits avidly, once when I was a teenager, and again when I had been hospitalised for a week while some varicose veins were being stripped. After a quick check of all the packages, it became clear that we had in our possession one novella-length and fifteen shorter adventures of the Baker Street detectives in the last years of their lives, all of which had been rejected for publication by Strand Magazine for a variety of reasons. One of them pitted the pair against the evil witch of Clapham Junction. Others treated pornography, rape and necrophilia. These were dark subjects for their time, but it occurred to me that Conan Doyle's later pre-occupation with all things supernatural – caused by the loss of his wife and son – may have been a factor in the rejection of the final detective stories, which, as everybody knows, should always have a rational solution, with no hint of smoke and mirrors, magic acts or spiritualism.

As I read on through that dark night, I understood why the first story had never been published within their lifetime. It concerned a series of quite appalling serial murders that, in the London of 1925, would most certainly have caused public mayhem and a possible breakdown of society, had it been fully reported in the press, or if Holmes and Watson had not finally solved the case.

The next morning, a quick phone call to a publisher friend of mine was followed by an early lunch and her excited validation of the first manuscript's authenticity. She confirmed that it could be published as written, with just a little editing to smooth out Dr. Watson's rather archaic writing style and even though its contents were still bound to excite a scandal among today's sophisticated readers, with their enlightened attitudes towards the story's central theme.

So here it is. Why not judge for yourselves?

John A. Little,
Portobello,
Dublin,
Ireland.
October 31st, 2013.

1. Sherlock Holmes And The Musical Murders.

Chapter I.

The First Murder.

I had thought that I would never see my dear friend Sherlock Holmes again after he departed the London smog in the autumn of 1903 in order to study the habits of bees in Sussex, while I continued my medical practice and idyllic marriage with my second wife, Beatrice. Our sojourn apart was interrupted by a single adventure in 1914, which I have documented elsewhere as *His Last Bow*. I then reentered the army as a surgeon, and served in that terrible conflict known as the Great War, while he returned to the safety of his cottage at Cuckmere Haven, on the southern slopes of the Sussex Downs. Or so I had imagined.

We lost touch with each other after that. When the war ended, I was forced to immediately enter a war of a different kind, as assistant to my own sweet Bea in her desperate struggle against tuberculosis, a fight she was tragically to lose. This left me a twice-widowed doctor with a dwindling business and haunted by some increasingly distant memories of a time of high excitement and derring-do, when I had recorded my adventures with the best and wisest man whom I have ever known.

But this vale of tears has a habit of sneaking up behind us mere mortals and shaking us out of our grief. It was another tragedy that brought Holmes and I together again, one that led to those marvellous last years of our lives, complete with so many dangerous new adventures and difficult challenges. For a couple of pensioners, that is.

Mycroft Sinclair Holmes passed away in his chair at the Diogenes Club on Saturday, February 9th, 1925. Heart. His masterful brow had, in fact, been stilled for about ten hours, but nobody noticed, as by this time his days were normally spent asleep in that same comfortable chair, his head covered by the latest periodical. His services to the government as a repository of knowledge were no longer required after the war. Despite being a Knight of the Realm and the Chancellor of a well-known University, he had apparently collapsed into a complete stupor, sated by hedonistic pleasures of a culinary nature. He had been lazy when I knew him previously, but towards the end, even changing his clothes and performing his daily ablutions proved too much for his enormous girth.

Thus I was informed by McNeill, one of the elder Diogenes retainers whom I happened to be standing beside in the Chelsea All Saints Old Church. Of course, I had hoped that my friend might have appeared at the funeral of his own brother, but try as I may I could not see him anywhere. As I gazed around the simple hall, I realised how few mourners there were – far too few for such a remarkable servant of the Crown as Mycroft. Most of them looked as though they might be retired Whitehall mandarins, ready for a similar service, and were simply paying their dues. Sherlock's brother must have been approaching eighty, and I supposed many of his colleagues had already leapt aboard the growler to that vast station in the sky.

'... ess you aynd keep you.

The Lord make his fayce to shine upon you, and be graycious unto you.
The Lord lift up his countenaynce upon you, and give you peace, both now aynd evermore.
Aymen.'

I have always found an Anglican service to be a certain cure for insomnia and had begun to nod off when I was struck by the tone of the clergyman's voice. Even with a faint Irish brogue, it sounded vaguely familiar to me, but for my life I could not place it.

He was a lean stooping figure with a fretwork of lines on a face that spoke of too many sleepless nights spent worrying about the state of his flock and the dreadful plight of the English-speaking peoples after the war to end all wars. A few stray fingers of white hair fought a battle for containment around his ears as his head wagged backwards and forwards in enthusiasm for his jaded text. He looked at least ten years older than Mycroft, and seemed to be passing time himself.

I cast my mind back into the previous century, struggling to match that high-pitched croak with a suitable candidate from yesteryear. A fellow soldier from the Fifth Northumberland Fusiliers, with whom I had served in the Second Afghan War? Perhaps a client of ours when Holmes was in his exacting prime? Or an unlikely reformed villain? Had Stapleton sunk in the Grippen Mire? Were Professor Moriarty and Colonel Moran really dead? What about that revolting blackmailer, Charles Augustus Milverton? A customer of mine, whose bowel disorder I may have temporarily ordered? One of my two wives' many relatives? No. No. *No*. It just would not come. And so I decided to approach this fellow after the funeral service, and demand that he provide some explanation of those deeply frustrating echoes.

He was standing at the door to greet the mourners as they filed their way out into the freezing fog of a typical London February morning, a regular pea-souper that might have travelled all the way from Hades. I held back until the end deliberately, enjoying the scent of the fresh lilies, so that I could challenge him on our possible acquaintance.

'Thaynk you for coming,' he croaked as I shook his wrinkled hand.

'Not at all,' I replied. 'Mycroft helped me at a time when I worked with his younger brother Sherlock, the famous consulting detective. I read about his passing in the Times. I had no idea Sir Mycroft had such an illustrious career. He deserved a better attendance at his funeral.'

'Yays indeed, but it's a cauld, cauld day. And does it matter, when he hays no dowth gone to a better playce?'

'Perhaps not. My name is Watson, by the way. Doctor John Watson.'

'Aaaaagh, yays' he cackled. 'Are you that same hayck who inflicted on a long-suffering public all them complaytely romanticised cayses, pandhering to popular taystes and ignoring most of the scientific detail I had specifically asked you to include?'

His voice had changed pitch and accent from the word *ignoring* onwards. Gone was the brogue, most of the facial etchings had faded away and a pair of familiar piercing grey eyes shone clearly into mine with high amusement.

'I most certainly did no ...' Holmes!' I cried in complete bewilderment and joy. 'Is it really you?'

'Hushhh, hush,' he muttered, glancing around and taking my arm. 'Someone may be watching. You must come with me into my vestry and I shall endeavour to explain. These are dark days, Watson. Mycroft was murdered, by the way.'

'Murdered, you say? But McNeill told me ...'

'Yes, yes,' Holmes said distractedly. 'The Diogenes Club would not want the truth to come out. There had to be some story, in case the dozy misanthropic members of the oddest club in London actually woke up and absconded in terror.'

He was sitting by a mirror, removing his scalp, with its few strands, to reveal a mat of healthy grey hair. This was followed by his make-up, and when he turned around to explain, I was staring at the hawklike features of my old friend, eleven years older admittedly, but extraordinarily healthy and definitely recognisable as he looked me up and down, grinning amiably.

'It would seem, Watson, that you have aged a bit over the past decade. That moustache of yours is as white as a full moon on a cloudless night. Why have you eschewed the excellent new motorised Beardmore taxi-cabs in favour of those filthy old horse-drawn growlers that used to delay us so much? Your practice seems to have dwindled somewhat. I notice you have started to read the Telegraph, a certain sign of aging. Oh, and surely you have not separated from your good wife?'

'Ah, no,' I said. 'She ... she died, actually.'

'Watson, my dear old fellow, I am so sorry. Why didn't you let me know? I had no idea.' He gripped my shoulder in dismay, in what he probably considered a comforting manner. I was reminded of my old friend's well-known deficiencies in human sympathy and his cold, unemotional nature. But then, how could someone who had never known the love of a good woman possibly share in the ongoing, palpable grief of a double widower? I exclude the inestimable Irene Adler, *the daintiest thing under a bonnet on this planet*, from my observation, of course.

'Well, we *had* lost touch with each other. I imagined you as still wandering over the Sussex Downs, harvesting honey and writing a complex monograph on the mating habits of different species of bumble bee. And just why are you disguised as an Irish clergyman at your brother's funeral? Good God, Holmes, have you made a Faustian pact with the devil? Look at you! You seem so damned youthful and thin, while I'm falling to bits. You're seventy-one years of age and you look fifty-one! I'm not going to ask how you knew about my hatred of those evil motor things, or about my work, as I'm sure it's something really obvious.'

'It is. You haven't forgotten my method, have you? It is founded on the observation of trifles. Although your appearance accords with your customary neatness, I perceive that your overcoat needs replacing, suggesting a possible difficulty with filthy lucre. Your shoes lack that depth of shine one normally associates with a conscientious wife. Those old carriages are beginning to smell, and unfortunately you reek of one. The Telegraph crossword is sticking out of your pocket. By the way, Royal Jelly is what keeps me looking and feeling healthy. It has many fine vitamins and fights the aging process. I must get some for you.'

‘Yes. Well, that’s quite enough to be going on with.’ I said, nettled. ‘All perfectly simple, as usual. I see you haven’t changed that much.’

‘Where did this disaffection for the taxi-cab come from?’ asked Holmes. ‘I seem to remember you owning a car at the beginning of the war.’

‘I had a bad accident shortly after that. Knocked down some damned silly pedestrian, who sued me for a bucketful of money. Sold the thing, and never want to ride in one again. Enough of that. Tell me about Mycroft. How did he really die?’

Holmes moved swiftly to lock the vestry door. He placed a finger to his lips, as though afraid of being overheard.

‘What I have to tell you will come as a shock, Watson. Needless to say this conversation never happened and you must repeat it to noone. You can never write this story up.’

‘Holmes!’ I cried, incensed.

‘Sorry, old chap. But it has been a long time, hasn’t it? Eh, have you ever heard of the term musical when applied to men?’

‘Of course. It means they can play an instrument, like you with a violin. Or a composer, I suppose. Singer?’

I was obviously on the wrong track, as Holmes kept shaking his head impatiently.

‘Let me put it another way. When you were in the army, did you notice any of your comrades who might be – ahem – interested in other ... men?’

A light shone dimly from a recess within my brain.

‘Oh, you mean, nancy boys?’

‘Yes, I suppose.’

‘There were a few such people, but they weren’t tolerated much, and had a pretty miserable time of it. Not their scene really, fighting and wars. Felt a bit sorry for them, myself.’

‘Well, Mycroft was ... musical.’

‘What?’

‘Yes, Watson. Mycroft confessed his true nature to me only a few years ago. He seemed a bit guilty about it, although his life was celibate by then. I reminded him that his younger brother was the world’s first consulting detective and had actually worked it out for himself. It didn’t bother me. He also mentioned that as a part of his active sexual life, he had once been a member of a group of free-thinking bohemian types known as the Bloomsbury Group, a mutual admiration society that used to meet regularly in a smug ivory tower in Gordon Square, over by the British Museum. You know, that ghastly Woolf creature. Free love, and all that nonsense.’

I scratched my head, not knowing what else to do. Mycroft, a nancy boy! A musical man! In effect, a criminal! As for free love? That sounded like an oxymoron to me. Love has to be expensive, otherwise it wouldn’t be love, surely?

Holmes removed his dog collar and stood up to shake off the two cassocks which had covered his normal clothing.

‘Now. You remember George Lestrade, don’t you, Watson? Well, his son Jasper has followed his father’s footsteps into Scotland Yard. He had heard of my exploits, and of Mycroft’s, and managed to put two and two together when my poor brother’s body was found on the floor of the stranger’s room, the only room where members and guests are allowed to fraternise. The details are rather gruesome, I'm afraid.'

'Holmes. Have you forgotten how you greeted me when we first met? *I perceive you have been in Afghanistan*, I think it was. A doctor does get to see the worst of all things, especially in a war situation. Kindly continue.'

'Very well. I'll say this once, and never refer to it again, except as the *murder method.* He was emasculated.'

'Good God! That's terrible! Eh, what does that mean, exactly?'

'He was blindfolded, tied up and his genitals were sliced off entirely and stuffed down his throat, with a wraparound bandage. He died from loss of blood. Slowly.'

I stood up abruptly, almost knocking over his table in my anger.

'Good grief! Such savagery!' I spluttered. Then turning to my friend: 'Mycroft did not deserve such an end, despite his predilection for other ... men. This doesn't bear thinking about! Holmes, we must find his killer and have him hanged by the neck until he is dead!'

'Mmmm. I have different plans for him, when I find him. It was an amateurish and messy business, so our friend is probably not a surgeon. Some form of knife was used, I suppose. Watson, the reason that I am in this unholy garb is not because I have suffered a late conversion to Anglicanism. The Reverend Thomas was happy enough to allow me to conduct my brother's service, which requires merely a basic reading skill, combined with a degree of gravitas, quite simple to fabricate. The reality is that I believe my life to be in considerable danger. Here. Read this. It was found by the body. Young Lestrade sent it to me this morning. It can be handled, as both I and Scotland Yard have checked it for fingerprints without any luck.'

Holmes handed me a sheet of folded paper, which I duly opened to find the following words, part of which had been cut from some bible and pasted to it, and the remainder printed:

Even as Sodom and Gomorrah, and the cities about them in like manner, giving themselves over to fornication, and going after strange flesh, are set forth for an example, suffering the vengeance of eternal fire.
Think on your sins, Sherlock Holmes, as you are on the list:
1. 'wttrdhhhtaweoeeyhpipraoosopntt'.
Love and bubbles, The Goatslayer.

I read the text through several times before I grasped one of its possible implications.

'Eh, Holmes. Surely you're not ... not musical, are you?'

'Hah! Only when I play the violin, old boy. Or enjoy a concert. No. Although I simultaneously worship and distrust the devious opposite sex, the only love between men that I can understand is the one between David and Jonathan in the Book Of Samuel. You know, one soul in two bodies.'

I breathed a sigh of relief. 'Indeed. I concur. I fear, Holmes, that we are dealing here with what the Irish playwright Oscar Wilde referred to as *the love that dare not speak its name*'.

'Watson. Far be it for me to correct you in a matter of literature, but that quote is actually from a poem by Lord Alfred Douglas in 1894 called *Two Loves*. It was, however, mentioned at Wilde's trial for gross indecency:

'But I am Love, and I was wont to be
Alone in this fair garden, till he came
Unasked by night; I am true Love, I fill
The hearts of boy and girl with mutual flame'.
Then sighing, said the other, 'Have thy will,
I am the Love that dare not ... etc., etc.,'

'Holmes, you never cease to astonish me, even after all our years together. I never heard you quote poetry before. You really have changed greatly.'

'There was precious little to do in Sussex during the winter evenings, and so I overcame my natural aversion to all things literary, and started reading some serious books. About other subjects, too. For instance, I am now conscious of the fact that the earth revolves around the sun.'

'But does it have a bearing on this case?'

'Indeed it does, Watson. Indeed it does. As you know, I am more interested in the workings of the mind, rather than the body. I am a brain, Watson. The rest of me is a mere appendix. Apparently our murderer is unaware of such details. He is asking me to repent, and that sounds like a very real threat. Quite apart from such trivia, there are certain elements in this case that are not entirely devoid of interest. Notice the word *list*, Watson. There may be many more murders planned, not just mine. This killer of ours is a vain person, who imagines that he is smarter than Sherlock Holmes. We shall see about that. And what about those apparently meaningless letters: *wttrdhhhtaweoeeyhpipraoosopntt?* It is most definitely a puzzle worth solving. We must find this Goatslayer before he kills again.'

My old war wound had begun to throb. All this talk of men with men was making my brain ache. If Holmes couldn't understand it, how on earth could I? Then it made me think of my lovely Bea for some reason, and the black clouds descended. I paced listlessly around the tiny room to ease my aching leg, which still contained the remnants of a jezail bullet fired into it by an Afghan warrior at the Battle of Maiwand.

'I don't understand it either, Holmes. Why isn't it possible for two men to love each other without any notion of romance, or some sort of disgusting physical contact entering the equation? Then we wouldn't have to worry about speaking its damn name at all. I'd like to think that is possible.'

'My dear chap. Of course it is. It's good to hear you haven't lost that pawky humour of yours. You never know, Watson. Some day in the future, the love that dare not speak its name might be more acceptable to society. And deemed less disgusting. As it once was in ancient Rome. Perhaps our flesh won't seem so strange then. After all, the New Testament was written about nineteen centuries ago. Now. As I cannot risk attending Mycroft's cremation, let us away to 221B Baker Street, with me in my standard counterfeit.'

Holmes picked up a red hair and beard piece, put it on, smoothed out the ruffles, shoved out his belly, bent his knees and transformed himself into a Somerset farmer.

'Ooooh, arrrr. Oi bain bet Miss Hudson hath readied 'nough vittels for thee an' me.'

I stared into his red face in wonder.

'*Miss* Hudson? 221B Baker Street? Have you taken leave of your senses, Holmes? Or lost your memory?'

The accent disappeared.

'Not at all. After our little adventure at the beginning of the war with Herr Von Bork, and while you were soldiering away, I was called upon by Mycroft to come out of retirement and help him with several petty war problems. I'll tell you about these cases some other time, my Boswell, and you can write them up as *The Secret Adventures Of Sherlock Holmes*, or some such lurid title. Once I'd published my own *Practical Handbook of Bee Culture*, I decided that I'd had enough of bee-farming – there really is a limit to the knowledge to be derived from their behaviour – and sold my cottage. I needed a place to stay in London and was fortunate enough to find our old rooms vacant. Mrs Hudson, before she went into her final domicile in the Freemason's Nursing Home on the Fulham Road, recommended her niece Lily as a suitable cook and housekeeper. She really is very good, if a trifle too interested in the opposite sex. You'll enjoy her cottage pie.'

He rubbed his hands together in glee and his eyes flashed with excited anticipation.

'Come, Watson, come. The game, it doth be afoot. Ooooh, arrrr.'

Devil, but I had missed him.

Chapter II.

The First Puzzle.

It is difficult for me to adequately convey my feelings as I limped after Holmes up the seventeen steps of our old hunting-ground, following a bone-rattling drive in one of his new-fangled motorised cabs, with their infernal combustion engines. There was conflict, right enough, as I recalled the bad old days as well as the good old days. Days when he was under the influence of a seven-per-cent solution of cocaine, and dead to all around him. Days when his violin spewed out a discordant, depressive wail. Days when he never rose from his bed. I wondered if his boredom threshold was as narrow nowadays.

'Here we are, Watson. Well. What do you think, old man?'

If I had been expecting something similar to the room that we had shared for so many years, with his chemistry projects bubbling away in a corner, the jack-knife holding down the unopened mail on the mantelpiece and a small rectangular box containing that damned solution, I was surely surprised.

'But it's so bright and clean. The air is so fresh. Oh, I do beg your pardon, Holmes. How rude of me.'

He had straightened up and was removing his false toupee and beard.

'Nothing to do with me. It is the fault of Miss Hudson. She moved my chemistry bench up into your old room, and arranged for the gas lighting to be replaced by electricity. Although it didn't want for painting to my mind, she had the decorators in last year. The rug did need replacing, I must admit. Do you know, she's almost as fussy as her poor aunt.'

While Holmes hung up our coats, I completed my audit of the room and realised with a pang that the only remaining differences were caused by the absence of my chair, desk and bookcase. The files, indexes, scrapbooks and bound newspapers remained in their usual places. His Stradivarius was still beside the telephone, his cigars and the gasogene. The Order Of The Legion Of Honour hung upon one wall, which also contained his numerous scientific charts. But the redecoration had removed all traces of the bullet holes which had initialled her Most Gracious Majesty - VR, from his efforts to relieve his intense boredom years ago.

'Don't look so downcast, Watson. At least the tyrant allows us to smoke in the room. Pull up the cane chair and share some of Bradley's finest black shag with me.'

He picked up his familiar cherrywood pipe from the coal-scuttle and his old Persian slipper from the mantel above the roaring fire and eased himself into his armchair.

'I think I'll stick to my birdseye, thanks all the same.'

Holmes was silent as we enjoyed our smoking. His brow took on its familiar furrow, indicating a train of intense concentration that must be pursued to its logical destination at all costs. He steepled his hands beneath his lower lip. I believe he forgot I was present for a while, until the rattan chair squealed in my efforts to get comfortable.

'Watson. There you are. We must find your old chair. I'm sure it's around here somewhere. I've just recalled a detail from my childhood, which might have a bearing on this case. But first, let us have some tea. Or would you prefer something stronger, to salute my elder brother's departure?'

'Tea is fine, thank you.'

'Miss Hudson! MISS HUDSON!!!'

A door clanged to in the basement. This was followed by the thump, thump, thump of heavy clodhoppers upon wooden stairs and a continuous drone that I could only identify as the muttered complaints of a young woman as she flung open the door and entered the room.

''ow many toimes 'ave oi asked yer to use the bleedin' bell we 'ad instawlled fer yer, Mr. 'Olmes? There's noffink oi like less than yer voyce screamin' moi naime for awll o' London to 'ear. O', 'ello, deary. Who migh' yer be?'

Miss Lily Hudson could not have been less like her aunt if she had been picked at random from a newspaper advertisement. To my tired eyes she looked more like a model than a housekeeper. Small and neat in stature, she had jet-black curly hair, bobbed in the fashion of the day, above an oval-shaped face with mauve lips that reminded me of the actress Louise Brooks. She had an ample bosom and wore breeches and boots, almost military-style. Holmes and I both stood up before we could stop ourselves. It's a wonder we didn't stand to attention.

'Miss Hudson, may I introduce my old friend and colleague, Dr John Watson?'

'Charmed, oi'm sure. Ye're the gent wot wrote all them detective stories, ain't 'ja? Oi read them in the Strand Mag. My auntie Martha told me all abaht yer. She said yer was quihe a one for the goils, an' oi were to watch moi step if oi ever meh yer. So oi'm watching moi step, Watsey. Oi've go' moi eye on yer.'

I'm not sure whether Holmes was laughing at the colour of my face, which was either a bright crimson or deep purple, but he certainly seemed to be enjoying himself at my expense. I decided that elderly dignity would be my safest response to this spirited young woman, who must have been at least forty years my junior, if not fifty.

'Eh, delighted to meet you, Miss Hudson. Those stories were not made up by me, you know. They were accurate renditions of Mr Holmes' cases. They were not fiction, but fact.'

She dangled a hand at me flirtatiously. Yes, flirtatiously!

'O', ge' away. Were there really awll them orange pips an' the six nappyoleons? Yer could 'ave fooled me. An' did 'e die at the Rykenback Wowterfall, oi arsk yer? Anyways, if Mr. 'Olmes is a detective, then oi wanna' be in on 'is nex' case. Oi'd be a bleedin' good sniffer, oi would. An' oi'd do it for free. Well, almos' free. Noffink oi'd like behher than a bi' of action. Wot 'ja wan'?'

'Tea for two, please, Miss Hudson.'

'Righ'. See this ov'r 'ere?'

She had moved to the fireplace and was pointing to a press-button bell in the wall.

'This 'ere's a bell. If yer push it, oi'll hear it dahn in the slave quawters, an' yer won' 'ave to shou' moi name awll the bleedin' time. Bell. B.E.L.L. Two teas comin' up. Will Watsey be stayin' for lunch?'

'He will,' replied Holmes.

As she passed by me, she stopped to straighten my tie, looking me in the eyes as she said, 'Oi used to 'ave a teddy bear loike yer when oi were lihhle.'

The room seemed to shrink after she'd left. I sighed with relief. There was a time, I thought, but sadly that time was long gone. Did she know I was seventy-two, I wondered? Then: there's no fool like an old fool.

Once Holmes had finally recovered his customary gravitas and settled himself on his armchair, it was back to the business of Mycroft's murder.

'Now, Watsey,' he said. 'I am expecting young Lestrade at any moment. I need to know the details of Mycroft's autopsy. He should also have a list of all the Diogenes Club members and guests for the previous week, although I doubt if the Goatslayer has been considerate enough to lend us his real signature. While we wait for him, I suggest we examine this note in more detail. I haven't had time to do so, what with my clerical duties. I'll get my lens and we should go over to the table.'

'Yes, Holmes, all right. Provided you stop calling me Watsey.'

His reply was a warm smile, raised eyebrows and a gesture with his pipe that promised nothing but further baiting down through eternity.

'First, what can the paper tell us,' he said, holding it up to the light and turning it around. There was nothing on the other side. To my mind, all we had to work with was the bible quote, and the handwritten scrawl, signed by The Goatslayer. But I had forgotten about my friend's knowledge of all things trivial and his capacity for abductive reasoning, wherein he would use existing facts to generate an hypothesis about unknown events. Several minutes had passed before he spoke again.

‘I spent some time studying the different types of paper once,’ he murmured. ‘I may even have written a short monologue on the subject. I can’t remember. Brain cells too damaged by all those years of cocaine abuse, I suppose. You’ll be glad to know, Wats ... on, that I have not yielded to the temptation of the needle for several years now. I am self-rehabilitated.’

So it wasn’t just Royal Jelly that gave him his energy. Noted.

He continued. ‘This is a common form of book text paper, used by the publishing industry. No watermark. The serrated edge on one long side tells us that it was obviously torn from a book itself. Which book, it is impossible to tell, although the other, shorter torn edge at the top suggests either a self-publication on a handpress, or a book that has been published in uncut royal octavo form, sixteen pages to a sheet. The size is, let me see ...’

Holmes pulled a wooden rule from a drawer in the table and set about measuring the paper.

‘I thought so. Ten inches by six and a quarter. This is the conventional royal octavo size. The paper does not have the same texture as the extract from the bible, which is thin, opaque and heavily loaded. So. A bookworm, bookshop owner, writer, publisher? Perhaps. Now for the Bible extract. What does it tell us about our killer?’

‘Well, it’s definitely from the King James Version, as the others are slightly different. As you have already observed, it’s the New Testament, the Epistle Of Jude, Chapter One, Verse Seven. God rained down fire on

Sodom and Gomorrah because of the depravity of their inhabitants and He didn't want the Jews to be infected by it.'

'Watson. I'm impressed. Don't tell me you've got religion in your old age.'

'No, Holmes. Just a misspent childhood studying the Bible closely, before abandoning it for a life of science.'

'So our pal might be of the Anglican persuasion. But the extract could be from any King James bible. There must be a few of them around. The message is clear. Musical men must fear the Almighty, as they are destined for Hell and eternal damnation. Usual psychological intimidation. It might be a religious freak.'

'Or it might be someone pretending to be a religious freak, with other motives entirely,' I pointed out.

'Good, Watson. Presumable relationships between musical men are subject to the same nauseating complications as those between dissonent men and the fair sex. If it were not for the 'murder method', that is. It suggests a hatred of the tribe, and their practices. Let's remove the gum, examine it, and see what's on the other side.'

Just then the door banged open and Lily clumped in with a huge tray, which she deposited on the end of the table.

'Tea fer two, an' two fer tea, me fer yer an' yer fer me alown,' she sang, winking at me. 'Wo' 'ja go' there?'

Holmes immediately folded over the sheet of paper.

'Thank you, Miss Hudson. That will be all.'

There was no possible way that either Holmes or myself would have involved this innocent young girl in such a sordid affair. She finally left the room in high dudgeon when we made it clear that her assistance was not required on this particular case.

'Yer jes' wai' an' see,' she said. 'The day'll come when the pair of yer'll need the 'elp of Lily 'udson. An' maybes she won' be aroun' then. So there!'

The door slammed shut, to be followed by a cacophony of hurried clumpings down the stairs.

Holmes took the lid off the teapot, held the paper over the aperture and waited while the paste melted. Then he lifted a pair of tweesers from the drawer and proceeded to pick delicately at the Bible quotation. Once it had been removed, he laid it upside down on the table and bent over to sniff the paste on the upper side.

'Gum arabic. Used in lithography, printing, paint, cosmetics and ink control. Edible, too.'

Holmes licked the glue and made a face.

'But not particularly tasty.'

'Printing and ink connects to the idea of the paper being used by a publishing company, doesn't it?'

'Watson, you haven't lost it, you know.'

'Yes, well. What about the quote and the Goatslayer signature?'

'Think on your sins. The word sin suggests Roman Catholicism, rather than the Church Of England, which doesn't know the meaning of the word. His message is carefully printed, even his signature, so we can't analyse his handwriting in any way. Now for the string of letters: *wttrdhhhtaweoeeyhpipraoosopntt*.'

Holmes stared vacantly into space, as though the meaning of the letters lay somewhere over my shoulder, on a wall chart. Now it really did seem like old times, and I felt a sudden surge of energy at the prospect of adventure and danger. The thrill of the chase. My friend seemed to have got himself a new lease of life. Why couldn't I?

He held the paper up to the light. 'There are no needle marks to indicate a pinprick cipher. As you know, Watson, I am an expert in all branches of cryptography. My trifling monograph on the subject, which analyses one hundred and sixty separate ciphers – *On Secret Writings* – has garnered considerable plaudits from around the world. Because of this, I was involved briefly in breaking a rather special grid cipher for the government towards the end of the war, concerning a certain shipment of arms to the enemy. Indeed, it may be that our work was instrumental in ending the conflict. That is not for me to say. What if this is something similar?'

'What on earth is a grid cipher, Holmes?'

'Well, it's nothing to do with dancing men, you will be pleased to know. We have thirty letters, so the grid might be 5*6. I'll create a simple matrix of the letters. Here.'

His nib scratched noisily over the paper. 'That's not quite it, but I think we're on the right track. We'll try 6*5 next.'

Holmes handed the sheet of paper back to me, with the letters from the message looking like this:

W	T	T	R	D
H	H	H	T	A
W	E	O	E	E
Y	H	P	I	P
R	A	O	O	S
O	P	N	T	T

‘I understand, Holmes. It’s really quite simple. This one reads ‘whwyrothehapthoponrteiotdaepst’, if I work from top to bottom on each column.’

‘Precisely.’ Holmes created a second matrix and handed it back to me with a smile of satisfaction on his face. ‘Now what have we got, Watson?’

This time the grid read as follows:

W	T	T	R	D	H
H	H	T	A	W	E
O	E	E	Y	H	P
I	P	R	A	O	O
S	O	P	N	T	T

‘So now we have the letters: ‘*whoisthepotterprayandwhothepot*’. This just sounds equally meaningless to me.’

Holmes wrote the letters out again and handed the paper back to me.

‘Now what does it read?’

‘Who is the potter, pray, and who the pot? Well, that makes for better English, but it’s still double Dutch to me. Although there is something in the Book of Isaiah about pots and clay.’

‘It is a quote from Edward Fitzgerald’s translation of Omar Khayyam’s Rubaiyat: *Who is the Potter, pray, and who the Pot?* The wine bowls come alive and ask: Did God invent man, or did man invent God? A fascinating question, Watson. Is he giving us a hint as to who he is? A sculptor, perhaps? Is it simply a clue? Does he want to be caught? Does he think that he is God? Talking of God, Watson. The quote is questioning the existence of a Supreme Being. What about it? Do you believe in the existence of a benign God?'

'Holmes, how could you possibly ask me that? Of course I believe in God! Don't you?'

'I have to admit, old man, that my childhood faith was thrown into disarray by that war of wars. What kind of God could have tolerated such slaughter on both sides? And then there's that Darwin chappie, with his theory that man is descended from the ape. He claims to have proof. It might well be true. I've always found it hard to believe that God damned us all because some woman ate an apple. Everything connects, Watson. And nothing has meaning. Our ideas must be as broad as Nature if we are to interpret Nature. Don't tell me that you have faith in an afterlife?'

'Of course I do. My Mary and Bea are waiting for me there!'

'Yes, of course they are,' he sighed patiently. 'You're a lucky man, Watson. Let's forget about such unknowable ideas for the time being, and focus on the quote. What does it tell us? Is it a cipher in itself? In other words, a cipher within a cipher? What kind? Or is it a form of substitution code? He'd need to work a bit harder on his simple-minded grids if he wishes to flummox me. And that word Goatslayer? What religion prohibits homosexuality more than any other?'

'Islam? And they kill and eat goats in the Middle East,' I suggested.

'Precisely. And with a certain kind of slaughter knife, too. Might be a clue, might not. Omar Khayyam was a 12th century Persian astronomer and poet, so that's another link. Let me see if my indices have any more data on him or his translator.'

Holmes retrieved a thick volume from his book shelves.

'Here we are. Edward Fitzgerald – born in Suffolk of a wealthy family – never needed to work for a living – preoccupied with flowers, music and literature – de-da, de-da, de-da – marriage to Lucy Barton lasted only a few months – very close to some male friends. Hah! There we have it, Watson. Reading between the lines, I think we may assume that the translator of the Rubayait was like Mycroft. A musical man. Is it a clue, perhaps? A clue within a cipher, rather than a cipher within a cipher?'

Holmes sat down abruptly and flung the paper impatiently down the table.

'Oh, I don't think we can get any more out of this note just now. More data is needed, Watson. We can't make bricks without clay. Now, unless I'm much mistaken, the musical door-bell has sounded, signalling the arrival of young Lestrade. Let us drink our tea while we await the unfortunate spawn of the bulldog George, who incidently passed away last year. May his soul rest in eternal peace, as his life was a continual irritation to his betters.'

'Holmes!' I protested.

Chapter III.

Jasper Lestrade.

'Mr. Lesteraday to see yer, Mr. Houlmes.' Lily, complete with faux-gentry accent, attempted a curtsy and failed, staggering back as she ushered a lean ferret-faced young man into the room. She recovered to close the door delicately behind him.

Jasper Lestrade sported a pencil moustache and twirled a homberg nervously in his hands. A visible wave of relief seemed to come over him when Lily shut the door. For myself, I felt that I was entering one of Mr. Herbert Wells' time-warps, as his clothing and general demeanour were carbon copies of his father's. A much younger version, of course, and without the sallowness of his father. For some reason he assumed that I was Sherlock Holmes and ventured towards me, hand outstretched.

'I am very pleased to meet you at last, Mr. Holmes. Most sorry to hear about your esteemed brother.'

I shook his hand cordially.

'How do you do, Detective Lestrade. I am Dr. Watson, Mr. Holmes' biographer. This is Sherlock Holmes,' I said, inviting him to meet my friend.

He switched tack immediately to shake the hand of his father's old enemy.

'My father told me so much about you, Mr. Holmes. Especially towards the end. All of it good. None of it bad. Well, he may have tried to match you once or twice, and complained about it to the family when he lost out, but I'm here to tell you that any assistance you can give me on the cases I have, would be much appreciated. I need help on this horrible one, sir, and that's a fact. I'm clear out of my depth. We all are, at the Yard. None of us can make head nor tail of it.'

Holmes cast a sideways glance at me, as if this were too good to be true. Either Jasper Lestrade was a genuinely humble policeman – a contradiction in terms, in my opinion – or else he was a masterful manipulator of egos. And he appeared to be rather better educated than his father, which I imagined might be an advantage to us.

'Lestrade. Please. Sit. Your father was definitely the best of the professionals,' oozed Holmes. 'He was a dedicated policeman, and a practical man who lacked imagination, but who knew his limitations all too well.'

Lestrade seated himself at the table, but kept his coat and scarf on. He seemed unaware of any insult to his father's memory.

'Yes. Thank you for your kind note on his demise. It was much appreciated by my mother and I. I'll put my cards on the table, Mr. Holmes. I am more ambitious than my father, and I believe that you and Doctor Watson can assist my career. I was raised on your exploits, and have studied your exciting cases in some detail. The manner in which you arrived at the solution that forced Mr. Jonas Oldacre to expose himself in the matter of the Norwood Builder, I found especially admirable. My father saw himself in competition with you, and was heavily prejudiced against what he called the interference of 'those Baker Street amateurs'. However, I feel that certain crimes necessitate a more circuitous route to their solution than are provided by professionals. Provided no laws are broken, of course.

Might I repeat my sincere commiserations at the loss of your brother, sir? This business must be very trying for you.'

'Yes, well. Grief has a way of disappearing over time, and during that time I shall be focussing on the capture, arrest and indeed, punishment of his murderer, this Goatslayer. Hopefully before he can get his hands on me. Any ideas on that?'

Lestrade pulled a slip of paper from his coat pocket and handed it to Holmes. 'This is the list of members and their guests who had frequented the club on the two days before Mycroft's murder. The Diogenes employees are written on the back. The autopsy report has been delayed, I'm afraid.'

'Thank you,' said Holmes, spreading the sheet out on the table. 'Why the delay?'

'Well, sir. The toxicologist discovered certain ... drugs ... in Mr Mycroft's system, and wanted to carry out further tests as to the presence of other ... substances.'

'Really? Most interesting. Do you box?'

'I beg your pardon?

'You look like a very fit young man. What is your sport?'

'Not boxing. But I do play some football for the police team. Association football. When I have time, that is.'

'Good. We must work closely together from now on, young Lestrade. You may have noticed that Watson and I are no longer in what is fondly known as the first flush of youth. We will need your legs.'

Lestrade looked pleased. 'I'll do my best,' he murmured. 'Long as it doesn't interfere with my duties at the Yard.'

‘Excellent. We make a formidable threesome. And you will go far in your profession, I assure you.’

I felt a momentary qualm at being included in Holmes’ plans without being asked, and somewhat nettled by his blithe assumption that I was free to join him on his cases. But he had observed all too accurately the paucity of my medical practice, and so my nature was swift to resurrect the loyalty which had kept me by his side all those years ago. If he needed me now, I would be ready again. And for my part I was happy to have some time away from those few patients of mine, with their dreary problems.

‘Do you have any data on the type of weapon used in the ... method, Lestrade?’ asked Holmes.

‘None whatsoever. It could be anything. All we can presume is that it is more blunt than sharp, because of the mess.’

‘But it might be sharp, and in the hands of an incompetent?’

‘I suppose so.’

‘Good. And can you keep this murder out of the newspapers for the time being?’

‘Yes.’

‘Excellent. Are you familiar with the terms of reference of the Diogenes Club, Lestrade?’

‘Eh, no, Mr. Holmes. Can’t say that I am.’

‘It is for the convenience of the most unsociable and unclubable men about town. There are many men in London who have no wish for the company of their fellows or their women. Yet they are not averse to comfortable chairs and the latest periodicals, printed on unrustling paper. It is for these that the Diogenes Club was formed. No member is permitted to take the least notice of any other. Only in the Stranger's Room is talking allowed. Three offences, if brought to the committee's notice, render the talker liable to expulsion. Someone who coughs three times can be expelled. My brother was one of the founders, and I have myself on occasion found it to have a very soothing atmosphere. Before I was expelled, that is. Can you tell us the time of death, Lestrade?'

'To the nearest hour, it was four o'clock, Mr. Holmes. A.M., that is.'

'Indeed. So my brother was murdered at night. Is the Diogenes Club open then?'

'No. But all the members have their own key, and can come and go as they like. It is possible that Mr. Mycroft fell asleep after dinner, and simply remained in his chair – as had apparently become his habit – until the arrival of the murderer. I have talked to Joseph, the doorman. He found the body at seven, shortly after coming on duty. He claims no other members were present then.'

'So it could be anybody who managed to get a copy of one of the keys. Not necessarily one of the members or staff.'

'Yes, Mr. Holmes.'

'I see. Now, the list.'

Homes smoked his foul shag tobacco intently as he perused the list.

'This is splendid work, Lestrade. You've managed to gather details about each member, such as age, occupation, marital status, duration of membership, address. I notice that two thirds of them are over eighty years of age, and the balance over fifty. The Diogenes Club should really start a membership drive, or else it will fold within a decade or two. Have you interrogated anybody?'

'Yes, sir. All of them, and the staff also. We spent the first two days of our investigation establishing their whereabouts during the night. All members are married or widowed, and their wives or butlers have provided solid alibis. Of the staff, only Joseph is not married, and the others have similar alibis. It would seem that the club is a bolt hole during the day only, Mr. Holmes. '

I noted with favour that young Lestrade was capable of irony, something his father had lacked entirely.

'Would it be possible for a day guest to remain there and hide somewhere in the club overnight?' I suggested.

'I checked that, Doctor Watson. Each member must sign a guest in and out, with the guest's signature included, in the Visitor's Book. None were missing. Joseph also keeps a record of arrivals and departures, and confirms this.'

'Right. Well, I don't think we can get any more out of the members than you, Lestrade. But we must have a look at the Stranger's Room, at least. I shall have to disguise myself as a senior policeman, no mean task. Watson can be my sergeant-in arms. Can you arrange that for this afternoon, Lestrade?'

'Yes, sir.'

I coughed gently.

'Holmes?'

'Yes, Watson?'

'Why would Mycroft enter the Stranger's Room with his murderer? Might he have known him?'

'Yes. I suspect that it is very likely that Mycroft knew his murderer. Now, the employee list,' replied Holmes, turning over the sheet of paper. 'Hmm. O'Neill is the only name I recognise. Perhaps their staff has turned over since my time there. I'd like to talk to Joseph, at least.'

'Eh, Mr. Holmes, that might not get you very far. Joseph is rather ... simple. His history is that of an orphan who was adopted by a pair of wealthy philantropists, who secured this position for him. He has been well trained at what he does, but I doubt if he can help us in any way. And although his parents were black, he suffers from albinism. He has no pigment in his skin and he looks white.'

Holmes placed his head in his hands. It was a gesture that I recalled from our previous life together. It usually meant that he was getting bored and losing interest.

'Gentlemen,' he cried. 'Without facts, we have no case. It is a capital mistake to theorise before we have all the evidence. We need ... information!'

'What about the note left by the murderer?' enquired Lestrade. 'Have you made any progress with it?'

Holmes indicated with his pipe that I should explain our findings to the young policeman, which I duly did. When I had finished, I noticed that my old friend had descended into the sort of silent reverie that used to indicate a profound concentration, but I rather fancied from the shade of sadness on his fine aquiline features, that he might be contemplating his dead brother and their childhood together. The only sound in the room was the steady ticking of the clock, until I became aware of a familiar clumping from the direction of the stairs.

Like clockwise, at one o'clock a grunting Lily Hudson banged open the door with her backside and entered the room carrying a sizeable tray with a steaming bowl and several dishes. She slammed it pointedly onto the table beside Lestrade, who leapt out of his seat in alarm.

Holmes chuckled.

'Won't you stay for lunch, Lestrade?'

'Thank you, Mr. Holmes, but I must be getting back to the station. I'll see you both this afternoon at the club. Three o'clock alright?'

'Excellent,' replied Holmes.

'There's 'nough fodder fer three, sur,' cackled Lily wildly.

Lestrade grabbed his hat and backed out of the room hastily. It occurred to me later that he might have gone all the way down the stairs backwards, just to keep an eye on Lily as she chased after him.

Holmes seated himself at the table, flicked his napkin over his trousers, and picked up his knife and fork.

'Hmmm. This smells delicious. I must remember to award Lily the fulsome praise she will no doubt be expecting. Tuck in, Watson. What do you make of young Lestrade?'

'He seems genuine enough, and a lot brighter than his father,' I replied, a forkful of pie pausing on its way to my mouth.

'Hhmm. *Seems* being the operative word. There's nothing wrong with being a careerist. Or a diplomat. I shall reserve judgement also, until we see how much help he can give us. Eat up, old fellow. After our lunch we must away to the scene of the crime. By Beardmore taxi-cab, of course.'

I groaned.

Chapter IV.

The Stranger's Room.

'Did you know, Watson, that Diogenes was a Cynic, who believed that personal happiness was satisfied by meeting one's natural needs and that what was natural could never be shameful or indecent? He was determined to follow his own inclinations and not adhere to the conventions of society. Living a life of extreme simplicity, he slept in a tub on the street and survived on a diet of onions. He became notorious for his philosophical stunts, such as carrying a lamp around Athens during the day, claiming to be looking for an honest man. The story is that he held his breath in order to commit suicide. When asked how he wished to be buried, he left instructions to be thrown outside the city wall so that wild animals could feast upon his body.'

'No.'

'What's the matter, old man?'

As if he didn't know.

'If you expect me to work with you on this case, we will have to find a different mode of travelling, Holmes. This hackney rattletrap is intolerable. And if you think the old broughams were odorous, then I rather think your exposure to Royal Jelly has destroyed your own sense of smell. For petrol and oil, anyway. And they go so *fast*. There are bound to be serious crashes in this incessant London fog. We could be killed!'

'I believe you've become a bit of a grump during our separation, Watson.'

'But Holmes, don't you miss the musical clatter of hooves and the screech of the carriage wheels?'

'No. Not at all. But I accept that you do, Watson. You are, after all, the one fixed point in a changing age. Ah, here we are. Thank you, Mr. Rees.'

He leaned forward and pushed some coins through a window to the cab driver. I caught a glimpse of a shiny, bald head above an angelic cherub-like face that looked far too young to be driving a murder weapon like the Beardmore through the dense fog of wintery London. 'My pleasure, Mr. Holmes.' The voice was a sing-song Welsh accent.

'Holmes, before we alight from this fireball, can you satisfy my idle curiosity on one subject?' I asked.

'I'll certainly try.'

'Why were you expelled from the Diogenes Club?'

'Hah! For talking to other members, of course. Three times. I grew bored and suggested to one fellow that he could sleep much more soundly at home, as he was obviously single and without family. Another objected to my assertion that his wife might not appreciate his intense perusal of the pearls of wisdom in the Times agony columns. The third was snoring so loudly that I simply said, *shush*. That finished it. Mycroft was on the committee that made the decision, poor chap. He never forgave me.'

Once we had managed to find it through the gloomy swirl, number 15 Pall Mall proved to be nothing more than an innocuous plain wooden door lodged between the more grandiose Atheneum and Reform Clubs. Neither plaque nor notice existed to identify the Diogenes Club. Far too exclusive for ex-army surgeons, I decided.

And Holmes seemed nothing less than a senior policeman, with his stove-pipe hat, black Inverness cape, bushy eyebrows and fine spread of bristling mutton-chop whiskers. He hammered his cane authoritatively upon the door, which was opened by a liveried doorman, dressed exotically in broadcloth, linen and silk stockings and with long, plaited blonde hair, like someone straight out of Harriet Beecher Stowe. Except that his features were purely white. His eyes shifted rapidly from side to side before focusing on us. When Holmes asked for Detective Lestrade, this throwback to another time and country, who was obviously Joseph, grinned continually as he ushered us into a narrow colonnaded hall, wherein Jasper Lestrade paced up and down, as though we were late. Which we were not.

'Mr. Watson. There you are. And Mr. Holmes?'

'Inspector Holmes to you, Lestrade,' said my friend sternly.

'Ah ... yes, indeed. I hardly recognised you, sir. Well. We can sign the Visitor's Book over here, Inspector.'

Once signed in, we deposited our cloaks and were asked to place socks over our shoes. Then Lestrade led us up a flight of stairs to a richly-carpeted balcony that jutted out in a semi oval shape from an elongated glass panelling, with a door at either side. I peered through this window at the strangest sight. It was like a monastery. Men were sitting alone in tiny cubby-holes, reading newspapers or sleeping. They were like wax dummies in a motionless ballet by Diaghilev, set to the gentle music of ... snoring.

'This is the main room, Inspector. I must ask you not to make any noise when we move through it to the

Stranger's Room, as all conversation is frowned upon.' Lestrade actually placed a finger to his lips.

We threaded our way carefully through the silent members, some of whom turned away from the intruders, until we reached a single door to the rear. This led to a small passage, like that between the two carriages of a train, and through to another door.

The Stranger's Room showed few signs of the recent murder. It was comfortably furnished, with book-cases lining the walls and a huge log fire that roared hospitably from within a wide fireplace. Comfortable chairs ranged in front of it, with periodicals spread across them. Two luxuriant aspidistras spanned the doorway. A longcase grandfather clock ticked away beside a wide bay window that looked out over Pall Mall. The bottom half of this window was delicately engraved with items of fruit and different family crests on each pane, against a background of fluted glass, which prevented anyone seeing into the room from the outside. It was flanked by a pair of step-ladders, presumably for use against the book-cases.

'Where was Mycroft's body found?' demanded Holmes, whipping out his pocket lens.

'Over here,' replied Lestrade, pointing to a small area beside the fire. 'He was bent over forwards, with his head between his knees. He ... he was undressed. He had no clothes on. Oh, and he was tied up.'

Holmes appeared disinterested in this news. I tried to imagine the scene, but without luck. My life with Beatrice had been a happy one, but I doubt if we had ever disclosed our naked bodies to each other. True, there were attempts to have children – several, actually – but they came to nothing, and after a lot of giggling, we decided to leave well enough alone. Nevertheless, I still missed our nights together, when we could snuggle up to one another for warmth on a cold winter's night. Enough. My leg was giving me gyp again.

'I see. And was he definitely killed here?'

'Yes, Mr. Holmes. There is no sign of blood anywhere else. We have checked.'

Holmes knelt down to explore the carpet with his lens. It was heavily stained with black blood, while the hearth and wainscoting were sprinkled with crimson splashes. Lestrade and I wandered about the room, trying to picture what might have happened there four nights ago. I was at a complete loss even to imagine Mycroft without his customary illustrious garb, and so I sat down and waited for Holmes to do his thing.

'Most interesting,' he said, standing up. 'The weapon, Lestrade, is a conventional farming implement, used for killing animals. A well sharpened slaughter knife with a straight blade twice the neck width is outlined within the blood marks on the carpet. The killer wiped the blade on it.'

He looked around the room. 'It seems we came through the only door. There are also the two doors on the landing, one of which leads to a bathroom and the other to the Main Room. What else is on the ground floor, Lestrade? Is there a basement?'

'Just the kitchen and restaurant, Mr. Holmes, with more toilet facilities. And a single guest apartment behind them which is rarely used, apparently. There's no basement. A double garage at the rear of the garden opens unto Carlton House Terrace.'

'And no secret doors into this room either, eh?'

'Not that we know of, sir.' Lestrade smiled at the idea.

Holmes walked slowly around the room, tapping each oak wall panel with his lens, checking, I imagined, for any variation of sound that might indicate a hollowness, behind which there could lie a magical passage to the street. But there were none.

'Hmmm. I'll check the other rooms on the way out. Now, the window'.

To my eyes, there was no certain way of opening it, or climbing through it into the room. The only aperture was a ventilation fan in the middle, with a long string attachment. Having examined it closely, Holmes climbed onto one of the ladders and peered through the clear glass at the top. First to the left, then to the right.

'A busy day in the Mall. Lots of Beardmore Mark Ones, Watson, choking their filthy fumes up into the atmosphere. And many nags on old hansoms, spreading their heavenly ordure onto the road. Ah, that musical squish, squash! There goes Joseph into Huggett's shop. He must have a sweet tooth. Quite a queue outside the butchers. Fresh meat today! Oh, well. If one wished to study mankind, this might be the spot. But noone could have come through here, unless they were invisible or disguised as a whiff of smoke,' he declared as he turned to step down.

Just then I heard a loud cracking sound, followed by the splintering of glass, and Holmes' body was falling to the ground off the step-ladder. I rushed over to him.

'Holmes, are you hurt? Holmes!'

My old friend lay still on the carpet while Lestrade ran from the room, presumably to chase after the person who had fired the bullet through the window. My only agonised thought was for Sherlock Holmes.

There was a significant amount of blood, but a swift examination of his body proved that only his left ear had been grazed. His pulse was steady and his pupils seemed normal in size. I concluded that he had knocked himself out when he had fallen to the ground. I sacrificed my handkerchief to staunch the impressive flow of blood from his ear, and waited patiently for him to come round.

Lestrade had returned by the time Holmes opened his eyes and stared up at me.

'Watson, we must find that chair of yours. Mycroft is dead, you know. Aaaaaagh, Moriarty, get away, get away! You evil genius! MRS. HUDSON!' He smiled weakly at me and closed his eyes again. It took him another minute or so to recover properly and realise where he was. His momentary hysteria had vanished.

'What happened? Why am I on this damn floor?'

'Steady, Holmes. Someone tried to kill you, and the bullet nicked your ear.'

He grimaced. 'Ah, yes. Our potter friend from the Rubayait, no doubt. He must be losing his touch.'

He sat up and I helped him over to a couch in front of the fire, keeping his ear covered.

'I believe he fired at you from across the road, Mr. Holmes. A couple of bobbies and I searched the houses and their rooftops, but we could find nobody,' said Lestrade.

Holmes took my handkerchief and held it to his ear. 'Obviously, my policeman masquerade was not good enough. He must have followed us from Baker Street. I believe that I shall have to be somewhat cleverer in my disguises from now on. We must keep our eyes and ears sharply open, gentlemen, as we are in deep waters. Would you be kind enough, Lestrade, to consult with the Diogenes powers-that-be, and see if they can rustle up a single adhesive bandage for me? Good man. I shall collect it on the way out, as we check the other rooms. And please send the details of the autopsy report when you have them, to 221B Baker Street. Watson, I believe that we can do no more here. It is now four-thirty. We might just be in time to catch the five o'clock showing of the new Buster Keaton film, *Go West*. The man's a veritable comic genius. We are both in need of a little humour, don't you think? Then afterwards, perhaps a bite to eat at Simpson's might be called for.'

Unbelievable. His life in real danger. Almost killed. On the day of his brother's funeral. Buster bloody Keaton. Whatever happened to Wagner?

Chapter V.

The Train Journey.

Despite my protestations, Holmes insisted on working alone over the next few days, without disturbance from anyone. He wished to apply his analytical skills to breaking the 'cipher or code within the cipher', he said. I returned to my practice in Paddington but found it difficult to concentrate on my patients' problems while my friend's life was in such danger. At night I dreamt of being chased by a herd of angry elephants up the Khyber Pass. I took this as an indication of my concern for him. That phrase about the potter reverberated through my head. I could make no sense of it in the context of Mycroft's murder. I even bought a copy of the Rubaiyat poem, and tried reading the section on pots over and over again, looking for some clue as to why the killer should send such an encrypted message to Holmes. All in vain.

I telephoned Lestrade, but he had made no progress. When I asked him about the autopsy, he stated that Mycroft Holmes had either taken, or been forced to take, a significant dose of veronal, a strong sleeping aid, shortly before his murder. There were also traces of cannabis resin in his system, enough to suggest that the dead man had been an habitual user of the substance. This was quite a shock to me, and I found myself wondering if any of us had really known Mycroft Holmes at all.

Against my friend's wishes, I decided to make a record of the case in my diary. I hereby beg forgiveness from any reader who finds my style somewhat wooden and lacking in pace, as eleven years have passed since I put pen to paper for anything other than a simple prescription. Where possible, I have endeavoured to inject some little humour into the text to counteract the horrible details of the killings. Also my memory is not quite as good as it once was and I am not getting any younger. Unlike Holmes, it would seem. I must confess that his example caused me to change my diet and to purchase a jar of Royal Jelly. For my own health, you understand. This had nothing whatsoever to do with Lily Hudson.

My mood lifted on the morning of the fifth day, when I received a telegram from the great detective himself: *Victoria Station. 3.30pm. Bring weapon.* At last something was happening! I rescheduled my single patient and spent the remaining hours in a state of nervous trepidation, worrying that I might be too old for the job. I searched for my rusty Webley RIC revolver, (it needed some maintenance) while wondering if Holmes had solved the Potter code, or if he had found some other hidden meaning in that threatening note. A clue to the killer's identity, perhaps?

Having braved a filthy day of shrieking wind and horizontal sleet, which almost made me wish that I had taken one of those damn cabs rather than a growler, I arrived outside the station at 3pm, not wishing to delay Holmes in his lofty work. But after forty frustrating minutes of searching through the restless buzzing crowd in the central concourse, I was beginning to give up any hope of finding him. Slightly relieved, I patted the ancient gun in the pocket of my ulster. Still there.

Loaded. Then I felt a tap on my shoulder, and looked around to face a strikingly decrepid old lady, complete with wide-brimmed feathered cloche hat, curly blue perm, brown mottled skin, rouged cheeks, bright scarlet lips and a colourful pince-nez perched on the end of a bulbous nose. Her fur coat must not have been out of storage for very long, as it issued forth a faint patina of dust whenever she moved.

'Excuse me, young man,' she said. 'Can you direct me to platform ten, and the four o'clock train for Brighton?' Her voice was shrill, tremulous and excited, as though it had been years since she travelled on a train.

'Yes, ma'am. It's over there to the right. Through the stile and ... the porter will help you then.'

Normally I am never rude to a member of the fair sex, especially if they refer to me as a young man, but time was ticking on, and I was keen to join Holmes on the murderer's trail.

'Young man. While it is true that manners maketh the man, I think you'll agree that plenty of make-up and a few old clothes maketh the woman.'

The hag actually winked at me.

'Good God, Holmes! Not again!'

'Thank you for your trouble, young man.'

With that, Holmes placed a coin coquettishly into my hand and staggered off on heels that were at least six inches too high for any woman, let alone a man. Only when I opened my palm did I realise that the coin was, in fact, a short note that had been scrunched up into a ball.

'Watson. The four o'clock smoker for Brighton. First class passenger car. Don't try to follow me.'

As ever, I obeyed the masterly chameleon, bought my ticket and later found myself sharing the first carriage of the London to Brighton afternoon train with a sprinkling of bowler-hatted City types, who were either reading the Times newspaper or sleeping their way home to the coast. Needless to say, there was nary a sign of Holmes, or Milady Montmorency, or whoever he was pretending to be this time. I was beginning to get the rather odd feeling that Holmes was dressing up, not to protect himself from some dangerous lunatic, but because he was enjoying it so much.

At least the scrawny conductor in his velveteen uniform could not have been Holmes. Far too small.

'Excuse me, sir. Are you Mister Watson?' he asked shyly.

'Yes, I am.'

'Well, sir. Lady Forsythia Moriarty, a rather ancient dear in the dining-car, wishes you to join her for afternoon tea.'

'Very well. Thank you.' Really! Lady Forsythia Moriarty! I was getting fed up with all this moving about and subterfuge. Why weren't we baiting a trap for the Potter swine, rather than running away from him? Attack, attack, attack! That had been the cry up the Khyber Pass in the Great Game! Those were the days, right enough. Kill or be killed. Day-dreaming of those wonderful times, and with my leg starting to throb again, I followed the collector dutifully back to where the grand old dame was sitting at the back of the empty dining carriage with a rug covering her dress and sipping tea in a most delicate manner.

'Do sit down. So delighted you could join me,' she murmured.

Once the conductor was out of hearing, Holmes returned to his normal voice.

'Who'd be a woman, eh, Watson?' he whispered. 'The fussy dresses, the reeking perfumes, the high heels, the make-up, the complicated underclothes. God, it's disgusting!'

'Holmes, I must protest,' I cried. 'Women are the jewels of our species, the very beacons of shining light in an increasingly dark universe. Without them, we men would simply revert to our animal nature, and return to the caves. I won't have you malign their sex like that.'

'Here, old man,' said Holmes, smiling tolerantly. 'Have some Earl Grey. It'll calm you down.'

'I don't need to be calmed down,' I replied, thoroughly nettled by his customary patronising attitude and refusal to take me into his confidence. 'I just want to know if we're safe here, and if you have made any progress on Mycroft's murder. What about that cipher within a cipher, for instance?'

'Have you brought your weapon?'

'Of course.'

'Good. I have my stick sword and knuckle-duster. Now place the gun where it cannot be seen but can be drawn swiftly. Hopefully our friend will have been led to believe that we are travelling all the way to Brighton. We will disembark at Haywards Heath at the last moment and pray that he does not follow us. I intend that we shall spend the night at The Dolphin. Tomorrow, old fellow, I'm hoping you will help me break the news of Mycroft's death to our father. I fear I cannot broach the event alone.'

'Your father!' I almost screeched, as I fumbled my life-preserver under a newspaper on the seat. 'But

Holmes, you told me your parents had died many years ago. Before we even met!'

'I know. I apologise, Watson, for having misled you on that. I'm sure there was a good reason for it at the time. If only I could remember it. The truth is that Teddy Holmes is a very frail, wheelchair-bound, slightly deaf ninety-eight-year-old who lives with a pretty young Norwegian housekeeper in the Sussex home that he moved to from Yorkshire after our mother's death. Ellie looks after things at the Old Rectory. I fear the shock of Mycroft's death will be too much for the old man.'

'But surely he will have read of it in the newspapers.'

'He never reads them. He is a total recluse, and has not received a single visitor since our mother died, thirty years ago. Apart from Mycroft, of course, who used to go down regularly. This is my first trip since her funeral. Good grief, how do women wear these things? My feet are killing me.'

Holmes kicked his shoes under the dining table and started rubbing his heels.

'Holmes, do you seriously mean that you haven't seen your father in thirty years? I find that difficult to understand. And have you warned him of our arrival?'

'I'll explain it to you later. There is a logical reason for everything, Watson. And no. It will be quite a surprise. Now, this damned poetry quote. I must confess my failure to you. Even after three pipes, I still could not come up with a single thing, other than the quote itself. 'Who is the Potter, pray, and who the Pot.' You do remember it, don't you?'

'Of course,' I replied. 'It's been driving me mad. Holmes, I do hope you're going to change your clothes before seeing your father again.'

'Hah! I'll do just that in the Dolphin tonight. I've booked two rooms, Watson, just in case people get the wrong idea about Lady Forsythia Moriarty.'

The twinkle in Holmes' eye did not serve to improve my mood.

'Well,' he continued. 'I spent many hours examining the quote for secret meanings, using my monograph on ciphers. I decided to approach it in several stages. First I split the text into digraphs, as follows:

WH-OI-ST-HE-PO-TT-ER-PR-
AY-AN-DW-HO-TH-EP-OT'.

Holmes noticed my puzzled expression and leaned forward across the table.

'A digraph is a combination of two letters that represent either a single sound, or another letter. A sound formed by a digraph might be 'ch' as in chair, or 'sh' as in 'shush'. In this case, I thought it must be a letter, as no sounds are formed by 'dw' or 'ot'. Do you follow?'

'Yes, Holmes, I do follow.'

'Good. Notice that no digraph is repeated. And the message is too short for frequency analysis.'

'Frequency analysis?' I was getting a little out of my depth.

'It's an old tool for breaking substitution ciphers, invented by Arab scholars in the ninth century to establish the sequence in which the revelations of the Koran had been made to the Prophet Mohammed. For example, the letter E in English occurs on average about ten times out of every one hundred letters. So if we had a longer message, with one digraph occuring that frequently, we could assume it was E, and work from there.'

'I see. I think.'

'Good. It is elementary, isn't it? There are many ciphers, so I decided to apply each one to the ciphertext on a trial and error basis. It may have consumed a few days of my life and come to nothing, but was rewarding in itself as an intellectual exercise. I tried the Mary Queen Of Scots, the Atbash, the Vigenere, the Pig-pen, the Playfair, the ADFGVX, the Checkerboard, all the other substitution and transposition ciphers, most of which require a key. Unfortunately none of these worked, possibly because I didn't know the key. I tried many options for that key, including MYCROFT, SHERLOCK, WATSON, HUDSON, MURDER, MUSICAL but nothing worked. So there it is. I must admit it. For once I have been foiled.'

'Wait, Holmes. Just wait,' I said loyally. 'Perhaps there *is* no hidden meaning. Maybe it's something much simpler. A clue within a cipher, which might be in the title of the poem, or the name of the author? What is a Rubayait, anyway?'

'It is a form of Persian poetry, I believe. Yet I hardly think that Omar Khayyam can be the name of our nemesis. I tried all possible anagrams of his name and came up with nothing.'

'What about Edward Fitzgerald? The translator?' I queried. 'Your father is called Teddy, isn't he? Surely that is another name for Edward?'

'Teddy. Edward. Edward Siger Holmes. That's my father's full name.'

Holmes' face had turned a ghastly shade of white.

'Oh, no. Oh, great God in heaven, no!'

Holmes had bitten so anxiously upon his little pen that it splintered in two. He looked like a stricken clown in his female make-up and attire.

'Watson. It takes a simple mind to discover the obvious. I have been too studious in my approach. Fitzgerald is my mother's family name. Now that is too much of a coincidence. It may be that my father is to be the next victim. And that our foe is one step ahead of us already. We must quickly to the Old Rectory when the train stops at Haywards Heath. And I must become a man again now. Excuse me.'

Holmes grabbed his bag from the overhead hanger and disappeared down the corridor in his clacking high heels. Any misgivings I may have had about his feelings for his father were banished as I witnessed his obvious distress at the possibility of injury or worse to the old man.

But what kind of fiend would want to kill a ninety-eight-year-old man? Then I remembered. *Who is the Potter, pray, and who the Pot?*

I felt beneath the newspaper for the comfort of my Webley.

Chapter VI.

The Second Murder.

A faint twilight edged across the horizon as we stepped off the train at Haywards Heath. The station was eerily quiet, with no sign of other passengers. I breathed in gratefully. We had left London's storm behind and the air seemed positively balmy in comparison. The stationmaster's whistle sounded clearly as I prayed inwardly that all was well at the Old Rectory.

Holmes rushed ahead of me through the gates. Pain shot through my gammy leg as I struggled with my gladstone to keep up with him. All thoughts of further disguises seemed to have vanished. Along with Lady Forsythia Moriarty, thank goodness.

'Hurry up, Watson,' he grunted, hailing one of his damned Beardmores. Placing my bag on the side of the cab, I consoled myself with the hope that the traffic might be less frenetic than London.

'The Old Rectory, cabbie. And it will mean a double fare to you if you can make it within the half-hour.'

'I'll do my best, sir,' grunted a pock-marked giant of a man, whose body seemed to stretch through the side window and onto the road.

'Have your Service revolver ready, Watson,' Holmes whispered urgently to me.

I patted the pocket of my ulster in response and settled down to a journey which I shall never forget as long as I walk this earth. The enormous cabbie was obviously determined to get his double fee, as he slammed his foot onto the pedal and we jounced our way through the village streets and out onto roads that had been built for country traps and not for motorised suicide machines. Each time we pounded over a rock or a stone I groaned, as my old wound ached abominably. Holmes seemed oblivious to my torment. He leaned forward on his cane, his grim haunted features a picture of deep concentration and the remnants of his flaky make-up giving him the appearance of an ascetic sunburned monk. Not for the first time, I found myself wondering about his childhood and family life in Yorkshire. Why had he become the insensitive adult detective, interested only in reason and logic? Had he been thwarted in love as a young man, and was that the reason he avoided female company so assiduously? Surely it couldn't have been that experience of being bettered by the late Irene Adler, *of dubious and questionable memory*? And why had he ignored his poor father for so long? I resolved that some day I would get answers to these questions, before it was too late.

Our cabbie excelled at his dangerous art, and we shuddered to a halt outside an isolated brightly-lit Tudor mansion after twenty minutes of excruciating misadventure. Fortunately he had managed to avoid killing anyone along the way, although a sluggish sheep may not have been quite so lucky.

Holmes paid off the giant and we hurried out of the cab together, through the white picket gate, along a stony, weed-filled path and up to a crenellated front door, leaving our bags in the road outside. It was slightly ajar and swung gently inwards at his first push.

'I do not like the look of this,' he muttered. 'Watson, the gun.'

I withdrew my pistol and followed him noiselessly into a low-beamed narrow hall.

'Hello?' shouted Holmes. 'Is anybody home? Father?'

Silence.

'Stick behind me, Watson. We had better check each room together. It's just possible they may have gone out for a walk, or to some local village do.'

His words sounded as convincing to me as I'm sure they felt to him.

Our progress through the country house was slow, nerve-wracking and thorough, but brought no explanations as to the absence of its inhabitants. There were no telltale signs of struggle or blood stains, although it was clear to me that someone had been living there that same day. Fires were dying out in the kitchen, main bedroom and drawing room, as though they had been deprived of coal for several hours. The remains of a shared lunch sat upon the kitchen table. A chilly breeze blew through a wide-open door to the rear of the pantry.

It was only when Holmes lit a candle and pursued a twin set of deeply rutted tracks through the mud out to the hay barn, that our unspeakable fears were finally realised.

The wheelchair lay on its side beside the entrance. Holmes stiffened, as though steeling his body for some terrible blow. I raised my Webley and steadied my hand. He pulled back the door and we entered the barn cautiously together. The flickering candle cast ghostly shadows around the walls.

'Too late, Watson. Too late. Oh, dear God. Father. I am so sorry.' Holmes' strangled whisper was strangely unfamiliar to me as it echoed throughout the barn.

It was empty, except for several bales of hay in one corner and the raddled naked body in the centre. It knelt forward in a large red pool, its bluish skin sagging, its blindfolded head touching the ground, its hands and legs bound together with grey bandages. From the wrapping around the face and the amount of blood, it was clear to me that Edward Siger Holmes had been granted a 'murder method' every bit as brutal and amateurish as that of his son Mycroft. The Goatslayer had beaten us to it.

I was about to rush over to the body to check its pulse, when Holmes intervened.

'Watson. We will walk slowly around the edge. There may be foot prints that we can use.'

I did as he asked, but the old man was definitely dead. For six hours or more, I surmised. While Holmes took off his Inverness cape and laid it tenderly over the body, I scanned the barn, searching for clues as to the Goatslayer's whereabouts amongst the shadows. But there was no sign of anybody, not even the girl Ellie, whom I hoped with all my heart had been fortunate enough to be enjoying her day off when the villainous murderer arrived.

'Watson, go into the house and telephone for the police. Before they arrive and clump all over the barn, I shall hopefully have examined the floor thoroughly. There should also be a note somewhere.'

'A note?' I queried.

'Yes.' Holmes' voice was dead. 'A note to tell us the name of the next victim, as did the last note. Except that I was too stupid to recognise it for what it was.' He took out his lens and scoured the earth patiently for footprints.

I marvelled at Holmes' calmness as I made my way carefully back to the kitchen, keeping my pistol cocked and a sharp eye out for any untoward movements. Once I had got through to the local exchange and asked for their Emergency Services, I started looking around for some sort of note. I had finished in the kitchen and was about to move into the drawing-room when Holmes returned, holding a thin slip of paper in his hand.

'It was stuffed down the side of the wheelchair,' he explained.

'Any footprints?' I asked.

'Plenty. All made by those wellington boots outside the pantry door. I shall examine them later.'

Holmes gazed at me with his deadly earnest heavy-lidded eyes.

'Watson.'

'Yes, Holmes.'

'When we catch this homicidal maniac, it is my desire that he will not be subject to the due process of law. Do you understand?'

'I think I do. However. I believe that you will feel differently when faced with the prospect of being his judge, jury and executioner.'

I had never seen Holmes look so dangerous. Yet I could not imagine him as a vigilante. His entire life had been dedicated to upholding the law, even if he sometimes allowed a crime to go unpunished when he thought that it was deserved, as with Captain Croker in 'The Adventure Of The Abbey Grange'. I felt safe in pledging my loyalty to him after these two great losses. And for a second I felt sorry for our nemesis.

'What does the note say?' I asked.

‘Oh, much the same as the first one. Except the gobbledygook is different. It’s probably a pigpen cipher, as it’s made up of symbols rather than letters. He just can’t help showing me how smart he thinks he is. I should be able to work it using some tables I have. But not at the moment, though.’

His hand shook as he gave it to me. It was the same bible quote, torn from another King James Bible, followed by the same threat on the same type of paper, and a similar set of incomprehensible letters which I could make neither head nor tail of. They made my head spin:

Even as Sodom and Gomorrah, and the cities about them in like manner, giving themselves over to fornication, and going after strange flesh, are set forth for an example, suffering the vengeance of eternal fire.
Think on your sins, Sherlock Holmes, as you are on the list:
2. ‘<⊓┘><┐□>⊏·⊡⊏┌┌·V>>·⊐·┘V⊐┘<·’
Love and bubbles, The Goatslayer.

While waiting for the police to arrive, I found a half-empty bottle of Martell brandy in a cupboard, poured two large glasses and sat Holmes down at the kitchen table. He fumbled with his pipe and shag tobacco. It occured to me that he was not quite as much in control of himself as he pretended to be. Of course I didn’t wish to make the obvious suggestion that he might be next on the list.

‘But, Holmes. Who would want to murder an innocent old man, and in such a vile manner? What kind of creature is this?’

'I don't know, John,' he sighed. 'But I do wish that I had visited my father more often.'

Holmes had never called me by my christian name in all our years together, and it truly shocked me.

'It's me he wants. Don't you see that?' Tiny sparks flew from Holmes' poorly-filled pipe as he drew on it to soothe his shattered nerves. 'Maybe I have met my match at last. It had to happen some time.'

I gulped down my cognac and poured myself another.

'No. I refuse to believe that. It must be someone from your past. Some villain you have put away, and who has been granted his freedom by some dastardly liberal judge,' I exclaimed warmly.

'Not necessarily, Watson. Not necessarily. It may well go back a lot further than that.'

He leaned forward and puffed thoughtfully. 'Oh, yes. A lot further.' His eyes looked wounded as he paused. 'Let me explain.'

It was then that Sherlock Holmes told me the story of his childhood.

Chapter VII.

The Childhood Of Sherlock Holmes.

'You may recall me telling you at the time of the Greek Interpreter business that my great-grandmother was the sister of Claude-Joseph Vernet, the famous French artist. She had seven children, six boys and one daughter, who married an Irish politician named Seamus Fitzgerald, a member of the United Irishmen, and a man committed to the cause of Irish independence from Britain. My mother was one of their three daughters, and was raised in an atmosphere of genteel refinement, with the emphasis on fine arts and literature. She became a decent painter in her own right. My father hailed from a long line of country squires, and was basically a farmer all his working life, who drank and gambled several fortunes away. I shall never know what they had in common or why they married, as they were like chalk and cheese. The family farm, Hillcroft House, was a few miles outside Richmond near Carperby, Wensleydale, in the North Riding district of Yorkshire. I grew up there.

If you imagine that I was a studious boy, Watson, with my nose in a book most of the time, you would be very much mistaken. My interest in the forensic analysis of criminal activities began later, while at university. Before that I led a perfectly healthy outdoor life, with the emphasis on milking cows, churning butter, cutting peat and herding sheep on the farm, as well as enduring many dangerous adventures with my best friend, Conan Arthur. Together we swam in the nearby ponds, jumped puddles, fished for pike and carp, played cricket and football in the fields, had snowball battles, charged bulls like matadors, fought as brave roundheads and cavaliers in the Civil War, acted out the roles of our parents, climbed the trees in the local park and drove the keeper mad by flinging acorns and worse down upon him. All perfectly normal fun activities for young lads.

Believe it or not, I wasn't very good at school. Passable at maths, subjects like history, geography and literature held little interest for me. I only read sensational fiction, a taste I cultivated from Conan in my early teens. Also books about unsolved crimes and mysteries. I actually had to work quite hard to get my final entrance examination into university. Mycroft was the real swot in our family. Although we never played games, as he was too serious, he and I used to go for these long walks, when he would explain his latest discoveries from the books he was studying and his shrewd deductions about the people we knew. I'm sure our parents wondered what we found to discuss with such intensity. My mind developed on those walks, as did my curiosity about human nature. And it was Mycroft who persuaded me to take lessons in the violin, to build on my interest in classical music. But he was seven years my senior and had already been swallowed up by Whitehall when I turned thirteen.'

Holmes paused to relight his pipe. His hand still shook a little.

'It was a very happy childhood, Watson. Both parents seemed to appreciate my carefree, fun-loving nature, in contrast to Mycroft's stolid, passive presence. This was in spite of an independence and lack of discipline they sometimes found quite unsettling. I was showered with affection and returned same in full. Then one day my poor mother had a flat tyre on her way to a meeting of the Richmond Countrywoman's Association, of which she was president. She walked back to the farm, hoping to get one of the lads to fix the puncture for her.'

At this point Holmes seemed to stall, as though searching for the right expression. Then he continued rapidly.

'Well, to cut to the quick of it, she found her husband, my father, the corpse in the barn, in bed with one of the farm boys. Jamie, I think he was called. I only found this out much later, as I was fifteen at the time, and presumably they wished to protect me from such goings-on. Mycroft knew, of course, even though he had left the farm by then.'

'In God's name, Holmes!' I interjected. 'Do you mean to tell me that *both* your father and your brother were ... musical men?'

'Yes.'

'Good grief. Thank heavens you ... Oh, well. Eh, doesn't this mean the two murders have been of musical men? So there may be a religious connection after all? Maybe a priest or vicar gone wrong?'

'Possibly. And father was once a country member of the Diogenes Club. I know all that. Trust me, Watson, these facts have been noted. But to continue. My mother was so shocked that she left the house immediately and walked back into town, where she spent a week in one of the fancier hotels. I have no idea what she went through then, or what compromises they made to fix things up, but they did. Probably for my benefit. From that time onwards, everything changed. They had separate bedrooms and their sole topic of conversation was each day's routine. What they were doing, when was tea, what we were having, who was coming, farming matters, etc., I can only guess that my father continued his dalliances and she learned to put up with them. I certainly felt the difference at home.'

'In what way?' I asked.

'Well, my mother seemed to take her unhappiness out on me. I could do nothing right and was under a constant barrage of criticism from dawn until dusk. My father never took my side in any of the arguments. Indeed, he gave me much the same treatment. They used me as a tennis ball they could batter back and forth at each other. It was a form of torture to me. The result was that I couldn't wait to go to university after three years of this .... abuse. Which was only verbal, by the way. There was nothing physical about it. But it separated me from them both for good and made me harden my heart towards all relationships of an emotional nature. And to distrust emotion itself. What is the point of emotion, Watson, if it is simply a facade for our basest carnal instincts?'

'Oh, indeed,' I concurred.

'During those last few years at home I spent most of my spare time out in the fields with Conan, switching off from that deteriorating family life. He had his own problems with his parents, who were devout members of an obscure religious sect called the Church Of The Loyal Brethren, in which he had been raised. Among their many strange beliefs was the notion that human life, in the form of a woman, had arrived on earth from a planet in a different galaxy, which they named The Birthstone. This woman, whom they called Rachel, and who was worshipped every Thursday evening, created a man using genetic manipulation and began to propogate the human race.'

'Sacrilege!' I spluttered.

'Just because they didn't worship a Christian God? I doubt it. At least they managed to avoid a Holy Ghost, Watson. Anyway Conan, being quite a bright lad, grew to hate the nonsense that was spouted at him each week and he left the Church when he was fifteen, around the time of my mother's shocking discovery. His parents threw him out and he took to living rough.

He built himself a small cabin in the woods and set up house there. I made sure he had enough to eat and drink from my own plate. We became close then, and looking back on it now, I believe that he might have wanted more from me, which I couldn't give him.'

'Of course not,' I stated loyally. 'Eh, we are talking about *the love that dare not speak its name*, are we not?'

'Yes, Watson. I suppose. Not that I was aware of it at the time, being quite innocent in such matters. I would head off to meet him there after school each day, and even undertook to teach him whatever few interesting lessons I had been taught, particularly if they involved mathematics, his favourite subject. He became dependent upon me, in a way that caused many problems. If for any reason I missed a visit, he berated me for hours in foul language. I was his only contact with humanity and after a while the isolation in the woods began to affect his mind. He may also have been experimenting with some plant he had discovered, as I remember him experiencing hallucinations. Once he thought I was a barbarous black savage, a cannibal come to eat him.

One stormy day in winter I arrived to find him naked, crawling around in the mud outside his cabin and muttering incoherently about having to travel to The

Birthstone before midnight, in order to save the world. I wasn't so young then that I didn't recognise a serious deformity of his psychology, so I had no hesitation in reporting his whereabouts and unhinged state of mind to my parents. They contacted the Arthurs and Conan was taken away in an ambulance to Richmond Hospital, a local mental institution, where he was to remain, I believe, for many years. He certainly felt betrayed by me, and I shall never forget his vengeful imprecations at me and my family as he left in that van.'

'So you didn't visit him?' I asked.

'No. Perhaps I should have, but a couple of months later I started my university course and became involved in solving some minor problems for my fellow students, which led me to the application of scientific methods to solving crimes and my career as a consulting detective. You know better than anybody how all-consuming that has been to me. I forgot about Conan altogether and only heard about him again when Mycroft informed me years later that my childhood friend had been released from hospital, ostensibly cured, and had married and settled down with a family of his own. My brother had bumped into him at the British Museum, just around the corner from Montague Street, where I lived when I first came to London. Conan was working there as a librarian and researcher. This was in the days when Mycroft used to attend those arty Bloomsbury gatherings in Gordon Square. You know, Lady Ottoline Morrell, or Lady Utterly Immoral, as she was known in the popular press.'

'Do you think that Conan has anything to do with the murders?'

‘I don’t know, Watson. He would be my age now and our man or woman must surely be much younger and more powerful to lift Mycroft or our father around. Not to mention overcome them and drug and emasculate them. But a child of his, perhaps? Who grew up listening constantly to his father’s bitter tales at the fireside of his betrayal by the Holmes family? Remember this fiend knows a lot about us, including where my hermetic father was living.’

‘We could check out any people named Arthur living around London?’ I suggested helpfully.

‘That was one of the first things I did, Watson. There are none registered. But family names can be changed, especially if there is a scandal involved, or a history of mental instability that needs to be camouflaged. It is difficult to find work after a spell in an asylum.’

‘The British Museum may have a record of all past employees.’

‘Excellent, Watson, excellent. A distinct touch of genius. Why didn’t I think of that? When we return to London I suggest that you occupy yourself with their archives, while I struggle with the latest cipher.’

‘All right, Holmes,’ I sighed. ‘I will. Exactly when did Mycroft meet him?’

‘Better check from 1890 through to 1910. The man you’re looking for would have been 35-55 years of age then.’

‘Right. What about your parents, after you left? Did they continue to live together in the same way? Just surviving from day to day and tolerating each other’s company?’

‘For many years they did, but my mother finally decided to do something about it. One day she walked down to the garden shed and drank a full bottle of weed-killer. There was no note. The family doctor called the act an 'impulse', as though that explained everything. It must have been an extremely painful death.'

I sat up sharply. 'Holmes, my dear chap. Are you telling me that your mother committed suicide? At a time when we were so busy together in our detective work? And you never told me?'

He took a first sip of his brandy.

'I apologise, Watson. What is the point of getting emotional about it now? As you say, we were very busy in 1894, and you had recently lost your first wife. If I remember correctly, I decided not to burden you with my loss. I attended her funeral with Mycroft and barely addressed ten words to our father, who had run down the farm through his rampant alcoholism and gambling by then and did not seem, I must say, all that bothered by her departure. He sold up shortly afterwards and moved down here.'

'But you must have been grief-stricken to lose your mother like that.'

'No more so than any other way. Five minutes, and it was all over. Many people linger in constant agony for years before they die. That is worse. And it is our destiny to become nobody's child, Watson, is it not?'

'Have you ever talked to anybody about this?'

'Yes. I'm talking to you now. But in my opinion grief is never shared. It is simply spread around. I have now lost my parents and my only sibling. I am seventy-one. Despite the way they died, one could expect to be in this situation at my age. Look, I believe that's the end of the story of my childhood, Watson. The part of it I am prepared to talk about, anyway. Judging by that siren, it sounds like the local constabulary have finally bothered to respond to your call. Good for them. It's just as well the Goatslayer isn't still around, isn't it?'

Holmes smiled cryptically as he took a second sip of his brandy.

Chapter VIII.

The British Museum.

I shall not bore my patient readers with the tedious details of the following few hours in Haywards Heath. Suffice it to say that the local police were suitably stunned by what they found, and were compelled to call in Scotland Yard, which meant young Jasper Lestrade, who arrived at the house around ten o'clock that night. Holmes told him what he knew, and Lestrade handled the rest. This included the return from a weekend away with friends of the fortunate girl Ellie, who was so shocked and hysterical that she had to be tranquilised and sent off by ambulance to a local hospital for the night. Holmes and I adjourned finally to The Dolphin around one in the morning, thoroughly exhausted, and grateful for our beds.

My sleep was fitful and its intermittent dreams were haunted by a middle-aged woman standing in the corner of a greenhouse, smiling as she swallowed a can of slimy green liquid, watched by a small boy smoking a pipe, his chin resting on his tented hands as he noted with interest the clutching of the throat, the body falling to the ground, the writhing in agony, the death throes. In the background, a shadowy figure in a white straitjacket crept among the plants, giggling. I woke up several times during the night, but could not rid myself of the recurrent tortuous nightmare.

There was a brief unsigned note from Holmes waiting for me at breakfast: 'Must remain here with Lestrade for further tests and funeral, etc., Suggest you return to

London by first train and pursue the British Museum angle. Would appreciate it if you could move back into Baker Street. No expenses to be incurred by you. Just until the case is solved, of course.'

Well really!

Frankly it suited me to return to London, as I still had patients to see, but I was annoyed that he should have risen so early and left me to my own devices in this way. I suspected he had other plans, quite apart from his father's funeral. Plans that excluded me. As for setting up my plate once again in Baker Street, such a departure from my normal routine would require rather more than a mere line or two at breakfast! Who did he think I was? One of the Baker Street Irregulars? Wiggins? No expense, indeed! Mind you, the thought of seeing Lily Hudson every day did have its attractions.

And so as usual I did as I was told, and spent that day clearing patients off my roster, and preparing to move back into 221B Baker Street. I still hadn't heard from Holmes on the second day, so I took his advice and started to investigate the previous employees of the British Museum, in the hope that we might identify his childhood friend.

After a hefty breakfast, I took a wonderfully lethargic hackney to the British Museum via Regent's Park. It was a delightful journey. Apart from the musical clipping and clopping, spring was in the air and there was plenty of enjoyment to be derived from the snow drops and daffodils. The fog had cleared early, the sun shone bright as a diamond and the sky was a welcome azure blue. Squirrels crept cautiously out of hibernation, realised their mistake, and crept back in again. I did try to concentrate on the job in hand, but found myself thinking of Lily Hudson. And of Tennyson: *In the spring a young man's fancy lightly turns to thoughts of love.* What a silly old codger!

I arrived at the Museum around ten o'clock. Montague Street hadn't changed much since my early days in practice. Holmes had lived there also, but it was only when he advertised for someone to share the apartment in Baker Street, that young Stamford facilitated our meeting in the Pathology Laboratory of Bart's Hospital. Somehow it seemed like a long time ago. What? Forty-four years or so? A lifetime for some. And a day I shall never forget.

The stern blue-rinsed crone at reception, with horn-rimmed spectacles raised querulously upon her forehead (I decided privately to call her Charity Pecksniff from Dickens' *Martin Chuzzlewit*) was initially most unhelpful in my quest. Until I introduced myself, that is. Then it was all 'Oh, Doctor Watson this, and Doctor Watson that, I've read all the books, etc., etc., I'm such a fan of Sherlock Holmes. Isn't he clever?' Indeed. Eventually she calmed down somewhat, and introduced me to the Assistant Manager of the Museum, Mister Archibald Eccles, a rather squat mustachioed curmudgeon, whose grumpy grey features had obviously spent far too much of their life poring over ancient parchments and manuscripts in dusty rooms. He was not a fan, but reluctantly agreed to assist me in my task. Grumbling away about the importance of character versus plot, a subject I knew little about and cared less, he escorted me into the Payroll Office, where all employee records were held in metal cabinets that thronged the surrounding walls, like sentries on guard against invasion by consulting detectives and their assistants. They were organised alphabetically, but with nary an Arthur in the A section, nor a Conan in the C section. This came as no surprise to me.

I spent the following three hours sifting through all the records, listing the names of employees during 1890-1910. Then I reduced it to librarians and researchers, male only, and of the right age. None had a record of any previous mental illness. No surprise again. Such details were not shouted from the rooftops. Not then. Not now. Probably never. I ended up with thirteen names. Inspired, I decided to talk to Charity about them, as she might have actually worked with Holmes' childhood friend. I swore her to silence about this list, which caused her eyes to glisten and her spectacles to fall down onto her nose with excitement. Miraculously, she remembered everyone on the list and was a fund of information about each, including possible addresses and phone numbers, if any. I was able to make copious notes. None of them appeared to have been born in Yorkshire, though. Then she informed me that two of them were still working at the Museum on that very day and offered to introduce me to them. Apparently the British Museum had a policy of continuing the employment of certain older people with special skills, for as long as they wished. I agreed, on condition that she allow me to take her out to lunch first. Has a woman ever beamed so much, I wonder?

Huge mistake! By the time lunch was over, my ears had begun to wilt under the pressure of Charity's incessant chatter, chatter, chatter, about her problems with Archibald, her ailing mother and sisters, the way the Museum should be run, her loneliness and the cost of everything from clothes to pens to cabs to theatres. I fought bravely to get a single word in edgeways. After a while I began to think that Holmes had the right idea, in never being too friendly with strangers, especially women. I managed to extricate myself from her verbal clutches back at the Museum, as she was forced to return to the reception desk. I am ashamed to record that I made a promise to contact her again, knowing full well that I would never keep it. Poor soul.

She had told me where those two gentlemen were located, so I was able to track them down easily. The first was an unlikely candidate for the post of Sherlock's mentally troubled pal – Jeremiah Ludgate, a tiny effete librarian from Sussex with a high-pitched accent that was as far removed from Yorkshire as Wales. It was genuine southern counties, with a faint hint of Somerset. And he was single, lived with his mother, had never married and would like me to join them for supper that night! I excused myself instantly, and moved over to the second suspect, wondering if it was now the 'in' thing to be a nancy boy, an alteration in society's values that had passed me by altogether since the loss of my darling Beatrice.

Suspect number two was more promising. Ignatius Doyle looked exhausted, his gaunt cadaverous face drooping peacefully back over his chair. His emaciated skin had the pallor of a dead man. He seemed to be sleeping soundly. However, he hauled himself up rapidly on my arrival, fingered his thin grey Van Dyck goatee protectively and stretched out his long legs. There was something effeminate about the movement. He seemed in a very bad mood indeed. Perhaps he didn't appreciate being woken up.

‘Good afternoon,’ I said.

‘O yea?’ It was a thin, reedy voice, his accent more London estuary than Yorkshire. His Adam’s apple jiggled up and down in his scrawny neck.

‘All right, then. Bad afternoon. My name is Dr. Watson.’

‘Better. Much better. Well done. And a bad afternoon to you, too. *Doctor* Watson.’

For a second I imagined that I had slipped into my unconscious mind, where all the writing action is supposed to take place.

‘Eh, I wondered if you might be able to help me. I’m checking on some people who used to work here between 1890 and 1910. I believe you were employed here then. It’s on behalf of my good friend and colleague, Sherlock Holmes.’

Another mistake.

‘Ah, yes. Let me remember. Wasn’t he the character who imagined he was some sort of brilliant detective? *Holmes, the meddler; Holmes, the busybody; Holmes, the Scotland Yard Jack-in-office*. Years ago, that was. Never believed a single word of those yarns of yours. All lies. Sorry. Can’t help. Busy cataloguing.’

‘I’ll have you know, sir, that many criminals have had cause to regret their contact with the *brilliant detective*,’ I stated loyally.

The loathsome cretin actually giggled as he turned his creepy pale blue eyes up at me and stroked his pathetic excuse of a beard.

‘But not all criminals? What about the ones he let go, eh? Like he was God Almighty? He misprisoned a felony on ten occasions, at least.’

'To whom might you be referring?' I enquired haughtily.

'Let me see now. Obviously this means I have read the books, something I wouldn't want to admit to my neighbour, but what about old Sterndale in 'The Devil's Foot', or Milverton's regal murderess, or Black Jack of Ballarat, or ... Ryder in 'The Adventure Of The Blue Carbuncle'? Eh? What about them for starters, *Doctor* Watson?'

'Holmes represents justice, not the law, Mr. Doyle,' I retaliated. 'These people were victims, not criminals, and in one case, he was about to die anyway. For him, sometimes the solution of a crime is its own reward. That's quite enough. I can see you have no wish to be of assistance to me. I'll let you get back to your so-called *work*. Good day to you, sir.'

Doyle slid his legs under the desk and continued his idle pretense of cataloguing. What a nasty piece of work! And worthy of a special tick beside his name. After all, the weed obviously knew quite a bit about the adventures of Holmes and myself. Could he be Sherlock's childhood friend, Conan Arthur, after a name change? Obsessed with his old pal's success in life, as documented by yours truly?

And jealous as all Hell?

Chapter IX.

The Second Puzzle.

Despite my doubts about the notion, I moved back into 221B Baker Street early the following morning. Temporarily, of course. It was another of those famous soupy London days, when you had to strain your eyes to see other people through the fog. Lily Hudson welcomed me down from my trap with one of her humorous mock-curtsies, pretending that she was in the presence of royalty. She grinned and fluttered her eyelids demonically while grabbing one of my two cases and leading me up the stairs to my old quarters.

'Blimey! Jes' movin' in for a li'l while, are we, Watsey? Yer cuddah fooled me! I'll betcha go' lead pyjarmas an' awll!'

'Is Mr. Holmes at home?' I enquired, as we reached the landing and dropped our cases. In truth, I had no adequate response to her challenging energy and levity.

'Indeed he is, Watson,' came a cheery voice from inside the apartment. 'Just finishing an experiment on paper. There we are. Most interesting! Well, come on in, old chap! Don't delay. What do you think of the room now?'

Magically, the chemistry bench was back in its rightful place, as were my old chair, desk and bookcase. And for once, Holmes looked like his old self, *sans* disguise, dressed in one of his dull mouse-coloured dressing-gowns.

‘So you see, Watson. You were not forgotten. We even have your old room ready for you. Miss Hudson will carry your cases up to it.’

‘Bleedin’ ‘ell! She will if she bleedin’ well can! He’s go’ a full setah cutlery in ‘ere, oi reckons. An’ some form o’ weaponry too, oi shudden be a bi’ supprised. An’ iron boots. Yer in the cavalry, was yer?’

‘Here, let me get them, Lily.’ I hauled the suitcases up the stairs into my old room, and was pleasantly surprised to find it almost unchanged since my last sojourn many years earlier, apart from the redecoration and a new bed. I felt that I was entering Wells’ time machine again, as I returned to the first floor.

‘Welcum to the mad’owse, Watsey. Ain’t it jes’ grawnd? Oi’ll be seein’ a lo’ more o’ moi fav’rite teddy bear. Cuppa’ tea, anywun?’ asked Lily.

‘Yes, Miss Hudson. That would be very nice. Never mind unpacking for now, Watson. Sit down in your old chair, fill your pipe and we’ll update each other on our progress.’

‘Certainly, Holmes.’

As he puffed away on his filthy dottles from the previous day, I reflected that this man did not look like someone who had lost both his only sibling and father in less than a week. And whose own life was in imminent danger of coming to its end. Even the story of his childhood did not fully explain his cold-blooded indifference to the normal, everyday emotions of the rest of us. His heart must have been chiselled from a block of ice.

‘Eh, what arrangements have you made for your father’s funeral?’ I continued.

'All done, Watson. He was cremated yesterday, in Haywards Heath. I insisted there be no autopsy. Ellie mourned quite a lot, I thought.'

'But Holmes, why didn't you let me know? I might have wanted to ... to share this experience with you, in some manner or other,' I finished lamely.

'Nonsense, Watson. You had work to do. Any word from the British Museum?'

I sighed, in frustration at ever understanding the lack of humanity in my old colleague.

'Yes. I went there yesterday and talked to two of the thirteen most likely candidates for the role of your childhood friend. Here's a list of their names and contact details. Ignatius Doyle was extremely rude to me, and it would not surprise me a bit if he was our man. And as a librarian, he might have access to the same type of paper that is used for the ciphers.'

I handed the list to Holmes, who perused it critically.

'True. I suppose we must check each of these out together, even though some of the ages are off the mark a bit. Dates of birth can be falsified, especially when it comes to getting a job. And I will probably recognise Conan, whereas you will not. Good work, Watson. Although Lestrade and I could find no further clues down at Haywards Heath, I have made some progress in the twin areas of publishing houses and ciphers. You remember Wiggins, don't you?'

'Of course. He must be middle-aged by now. Surely he's not still doing odd jobs for you?'

'As well as ever. Although he operates alone, the other Baker Street Irregulars having gone their separate ways, including several into the hands of Her Majesty's Prison Service, I regret to report. And he costs somewhat more than a shilling nowadays. I asked him to purchase samples of the type of paper used by a list of London publishers. I then compared them under the lens with the paper used by our friend, and guess what?'

'I give up, Holmes. What?'

'I found one exact match. And it was particularly interesting. Have you heard of the Hogarth Press?'

'No. They must be a small or private Publishing House.'

'Watson, what would you say if I were to tell you that the Hogarth Press is run by Virginia Woolf and her husband Leonard, to publish the Bloomsbury Group's own appallingly tedious novels and poetry?'

Holmes' body language resembled that of a magician pulling a rabbit out of a hat. It had the desired effect on me.

'Oh, well done. I'd say we were onto something concrete at last, Holmes. Mycroft was a member of the Group, and they are known for their sexual ... laxity.'

'Well. All it really means is that the killer has access to the same type of paper used by the Group. He might have purchased some of their books, and may not have anything to do with that lot. And the fact that Mycroft was once a member may be pure coincidence.'

'But Holmes, put that with the notion of free love and musical men. That's a definite connection. Also the first clue was of a literary nature. What about the second clue? Have you solved it yet?'

'I believe so. But I'm not sure it gets us very far. As I thought, it is a simple pigpen cipher. Our man is no mathematical genius. Indeed, his mind is quite childish. He seems to be learning as he goes along.'

‘What exactly is a pigpen cipher, Holmes?’ It occurred to me that sometimes I could be confused with the straight man in a comedy duo, feeding the funny man his lines.

‘It’s a substitution code, where symbols are swapped with letters, based on a grid. Other names for it are the tic-tac-toe or masonic cipher. The scheme was developed by Freemasons in the early 1700s for record-keeping and correspondence, and was used by the Confederates in the American Civil War. The grid can be any agreed set of symbols, but the most commonly used one is a box-and-dot, like this one.

Holmes handed me a piece of paper with this puzzling diagram drawn upon it:

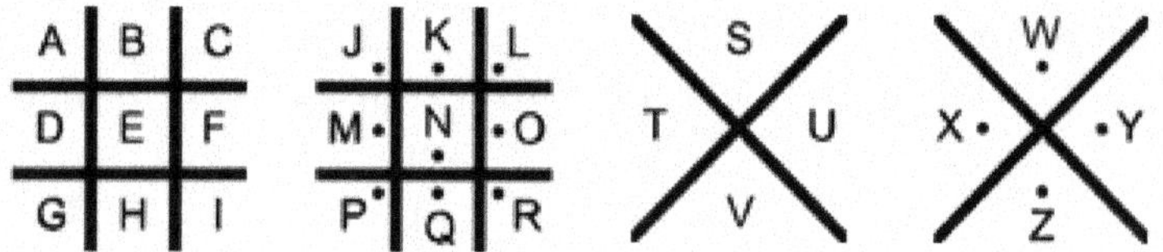

‘In other words, Watson,

a= ⅃ , b = ⊔ , c = L , d = ⊐ and so on, right down to z = ∧ .

This can be personalised by entry of an agreed keyword at the beginning, thereby creating a unique substitution code. Each symbol can be shifted to a different angle, say ninety degress, to make any decryption more complex. Or indeed, any equation of letters to any set of symbols can be agreed in advance of encryption. I’m sure you get my meaning. Anyway, using the conventional method of transposing the letters for the symbols:

< ⊓ ⅃ > < ˥ ☐ > ⊏ ⊡ ⊏ Γ Γ V > > ⊐ ⅃ V ⊐ ⅃ <

translates to:

W.H.A.T. U. G.E.T. O.N. F.I.R.S.T. X.M.A.S. D.A.Y.

Now what do you make of that, Watson?'

'Not a single thing. I can't think at the moment. My head's not right, and my brain hurts. Eh. Presents? Santa Claus? Turkey? Drunk?'

'First, Watson. What u get on *first* xmas day. Hhmm. I confess it has caused me some puzzlement also. More pipes might be needed.'

'A bleedin' par'ridge in a bleedin' pear tree, tha's woh!'

We were so involved with the cipher that we had failed to notice Lily Hudson entering the room with her tray.

'Oi tol' yer pair the day'd come when yer'd need the 'elp o' Lily 'udson. An' oi were righ'!'

I leapt out of my chair with excitement. Well, almost.

'Of course. What a clever girl, Lily! She's absolutely on the button, Holmes. You are familiar with the Christmas Song, aren't you?'

I burst into the first few verses of the song, with Lily joining in, for good measure:

'On the first day of Christmas,
my true love sent to me
A partridge in a pear tree.
On the second day of Christmas,
my true love sent to me
Two turtle doves,
And a partridge in a pear tree.
On the third day of Christmas,
my true love sent to me ...'

‘Enough! Good God! Do stop!’ shouted Holmes, jumping up also.

‘A partridge in a pear tree, Holmes. Don’t you see? That’s the clue!’

‘Yes, yes, Watson. I do get it. I’m not entirely dense, you know. And apparently my present housekeeper is almost as intelligent as I.

‘But what does it mean?’ I mused. ‘Thank you, Lily.’

Lily poured our tea silently for us, and left the room quietly, and I suspect, rather hurt by her master’s threatening lack of enthusiasm for her efforts.

‘I say, Holmes. You were a bit rough on her. Just because she showed us both up.’

‘Yes, yes, Watson. But what does that line mean? Where is the clue? Partridge, pear and tree are the only nouns in it, so presumably it might mean that the name of the next victim is one of those.’

‘What can we do about it? Find everyone with those names, and warn them?’

‘We can but try. Fetch me the directory, will you?’

‘Eh, where is it kept now?’ I asked innocently.

‘On the mantelpiece, beside the telephone.’

‘Oh, I see. Same place as usual. I had forgotten. Here you are, Holmes.’

Holmes opened the directory on the table and flicked through the pages.

‘Now let’s see ... Peak, Peal, Pean, Peas ... no Pear ... Treber, Trecine, Tredwell ... no Tree ... Partridge, Partridge, Partridge. There are three Partridges in the London book, so I suggest that we start there. Damn. Who can that be at this hour of the day?’

Noisy clumpings from the stairs signalled Lily’s arrival after the bell. She was followed closely by an obviously stressed-out Jasper Lestrade, who burst past her into the room, gesturing frantically with his hat.

'There's been another murder,' he blurted.

'Great Heavens! Who the devil is it?' Holmes and I shouted in unison.

'Reginald Sherring Partridge. Apparently he was a writer of sorts.'

Chapter X.

The Third Murder.

The effect of these words on my old friend was truly dramatic. He slumped into a chair and placed his head in his hands, like someone who has just learned he has three weeks to live. I imagined that he was upset because of our delay in breaking the pigpen cipher and the possible prevention of this last murder. After all, we might have saved a life. But I was wrong. It was relief.

Holmes recovered his nerve quickly and looked up in puzzlement at Lestrade.

'Sit down, man. Where did this happen and when? And is it the same murder ... method?'

Lestrade threw his hat onto the table and slid onto a chair in exhaustion.

'Excuse me, gentlemen,' he said. 'But I have been up all night on this latest case, and it has come so soon after the previous one in Haywards Heath. I need a moment to compose myself.'

'Watson, the brandy.'

'Of course, Holmes.'

Lestrade swigged a couple of fingers greedily, leaned back and started to talk.

'Yes. It was exactly the same kind of murder, with the same position of the body, and the same sort of ... condition.'

'Wha' condition were tha', then?'

We had forgotten that Lily was still there.

'Thank you, Miss Hudson. That will be all.'

Holmes was adamant about this, although I was beginning to think that we might need Lily's intuition, if only to supplement Holmes' razor-like logic and my shambling efforts. I had come to the conclusion that her jokey exterior masked an intelligent, questioning mind. She was really quite bright.

Lestrade continued above the grumbling from the stairs.

'Eh, not entirely the same condition, Mr. Holmes. There was nothing stuffed down his throat this time. The killers must have taken the ... bits and bobs ... away with them.'

'Killers?' queried Holmes.

'Yes. Mr. Partridge had quite a large build. I think we may have to consider the possibility of there being two people involved in these murders, in order for a sedative to be successfully applied.'

'There was only one set of footprints in Haywards Heath,' said Holmes. 'But I take your point. Perhaps they were interrupted in their work, and did not have enough time to fulfill the ritual mutilation. Where did all this happen?'

'Mr. Partridge was staying with some friends in 41 Gordon Square, over near the British Museum. A Mr. James Strachey and his wife, Alix, who discovered him in their basement last evening, upon returning from a day out. He was still alive, but unconscious, and died before medical assistance could arrive. Apparently he normally resided in Berkshire, with his own wife and Mr. Strachey's brother. What?'

Lestrade had observed the look exchanged between Holmes and myself.

At this point Holmes updated Lestrade with our findings from the second cipher, and the warning contained in the name Partridge, without mentioning his childhood friend or my visit to the British Museum. I shuddered at the idea of another, similar murder being carried out so near to where I had spent most of the previous day. Yet it seemed somehow that we were getting closer to the murderer. Or he was getting closer to us.

Lestrade was particularly interested in the connection with the Hogarth Press.

'Now that is something concrete, which I can follow up. Mrs Woolf and her coterie are well known to Scotland Yard, mainly due to complaints from their neighbours in Tavistock Square about late night parties and other shenanigans.'

Holmes filled his pipe with fresh tobacco, and set it alight with a coal from the fire.

'The Bloomsbury Group, I believe they are called, detective,' suggested Holmes. 'After the London area they live in. This man Partridge may have been a member of the gang. They are a set of bohemian artistes and intellectuals who might consider themselves to be above the bourgeois law that governs the lives of us ordinary folk.'

Lestrade extricated a tiny yellow notebook from his pocket and scribbled down some details.

'So what do we have, gentlemen?' continued Holmes. 'Two members of my family murdered, both musical men who were members of the Diogenes Club, followed by a writer called Partridge, who may or may not have had something to do with the Bloomsbury Group. And who also may, or may not have been a musical man, living in a *menage a trois* in Berkshire. Yes?'

'What in the name of all Jehovah is a *menage a trois*, Holmes?' I asked.

'A man living with two women, or a woman living with two men.'

'Or a man living with a man and a woman,' interjected Lestrade.

'Great Heavens above,' I said. 'Do you mean, sharing beds? Three in a bed?'

'Not necessarily, Watson. Not at the same time, that is.'

'Oh, that is such a relief. Sounds a bit like musical chairs.'

For someone whose sexual experiences had fallen considerably beneath the radar of a twice-married man like myself, Holmes really was pushing it a bit, behaving as though he himself had once been a member of a *menage a trois* and knew all about the thing. I doubted that he had ever been a member of a *menage a deux*. Certainly not with Irene Adler. But I decided to keep my mouth shut on the subject of such complicated human liaisons for the time being.

'Actually, gentlemen,' said Lestrade. 'According to James Strachey and his wife, Reginald – he was known as Ralph, by the way – Partridge was *not* a musical man. The situation down at Mill House in Berkshire, is a complicated one. His wife is a painter called Dorothy ...'

Here Lestrade consulted his notebook.

'... Carrington. She is in love with James' brother, Lytton, who lives with her and Partridge. He is also a writer and a musical man, who was in love with Ralph

Partridge. Unrequited love, that is. As is hers for this Lytton fellow. Hhhmm. Yes. I think I've got that right.'

'Most interesting,' burst out Holmes. 'So our friend may have made a mistake in his choice of victim. I wonder why. Or does he know something about this situation that we do not? Look here. We must establish firmly whether or not Mr. Partridge was musical and if he was also a member of the Diogenes Club. And how the killer entered the premises, of course. I'm not sure that Watson and I need to examine yet another victim in the same appalling state. We will visit Mr. James Strachey's house, however. And then we have some other fish to fry. Isn't that right, Watson?'

'Oh, yes. Indeed, Holmes.' It occured to me that I had not yet had my breakfast, being in too much of a hurry to move digs. And kippers sounded good.

'Detective Lestrade. Can you continue to keep these murders out of the daily rags?'

'I think so, but not for much longer.'

'Good. Was there another note with the body?'

'Yes. Here it is, Mr. Holmes. I cannot make any sense of it.'

Lestrade handed a paper to Holmes, who studied it briefly and passed it over to me, commenting: 'Looks like a Vigenère cipher, and I imagine we must break it fairly quickly, if we wish to save the next victim. This must be our first priority.'

I read the same message for the third time, with yet another cipher/clue inserted:

Even as Sodom and Gomorrah, and the cities about them in like manner, giving themselves over to

fornication, and going after strange flesh, are set forth for an example, suffering the vengeance of eternal fire. Think on your sins, Sherlock Holmes, as you are on the list:
3. 'gfhkuedixhxpnzvlyrspmpgvtvla'.
Love and bubbles, The Goatslayer.

'He might be a Russian,' I suggested, handing it back to him.

'Surely we must try to discover the link between this murder, and the two previous ones?' suggested Lestrade, helping himself to another slug of brandy. 'After all, Mr. Partridge isn't your long-lost brother, born outside the blanket, is he, Mr. Holmes?'

Holmes didn't answer. He had lapsed into that near-catatonic state that usually indicated some deep process of ratiocination. Whereas I was used to his periodic comas, young Lestrade grew increasingly impatient. After a while he put on his gloves and grabbed his hat.

Eventually the fog cleared, the body moved and Holmes spoke.

'What? Oh. Not that I know of, anyway. And I'm not sure what happened outside the blanket, Lestrade, as you so delicately put it.' He drummed his fingers on the table, as though seeking inspiration from the rhythm.

Lestrade stood up.

'I shall visit Mrs Woolf and then return to Scotland Yard and fill out the usual paperwork. There'll have to be another autopsy. No doubt it will confirm the presence of veronal, as it did in the case of your brother. Then hopefully I might gain a few hours sleep. I will be available from late afternoon onwards, if you should need me, Mr. Holmes. Goodbye, Dr. Watson.'

‘Goodbye, Lestrade.’ Holmes continued to drum, seemingly unaware of the young detective’s departure.

Lestrade descended the stairs rapidly, no doubt wishing to avoid a collision with Lily Hudson.

The drumming ceased.

‘Watson, we must act with more speed this time. Our friend seems to be always one step ahead of us. If I didn’t know you better, I might even begin to suspect you.’

‘Holmes! How could you! What a thing to say!’

‘I’m sorry, old man. It was just a little joke of mine, utterly facetious and inexcusable. Will you forgive me?’

‘Oh, well. All right. But let’s work together from now on, not separately, as we have been doing. I believe that we have always worked better when our two minds are focused on a particular crime. I also believe that we should begin to include Lily in our undertakings.’

‘Lily? But I thought you wanted to protect her from these vile crimes?’

‘I don’t mean that she should play an active part, Holmes. I wouldn’t want to expose her to any danger. Certainly not. It’s just that she has a different viewpoint on life, and may know more about these types of crimes and their perpetrators than we realise.’

‘I can’t accept that she would know anything about serial killers of so-called musical men, Watson. However, I agree. Provided she continues to bring me my tea and meals when I want them.’

‘Good. Which reminds me. Have you had breakfast yet?’

‘No. An excellent idea, Watson. And this also provides an opportunity to use Lily’s precious bell for the first time.’

Holmes leaned back in his chair, picked up his stick sword and used it to press the bell.

'In the meantime, we must address our minds to the problem of the Vigenère cipher and find the name of the next victim. Sit over here beside me.'

'Oh, well. If I must, Holmes.'

Chapter XI.

The Third Puzzle.

'The Vigenère cipher is a polyalphabetic cipher. It uses twenty-six different alphabetic sequences, each shifted successively by one letter to the right – called a Caesar shift after old Julius won some battle with it – and a keyword to move between them. This cipher was first broken by a chap named Charles Babbage using an invention called the Analytical Engine, an effective device that may have a decent future. The problem with breaking it lies in finding the keyword showing which lines in the alphabet sequence to use. This might make it clearer.'

Holmes delved into a drawer in the table, rummaged around a bit, withdrew a document and handed it to me:

	A	B	C	D	E	F	G	H	I	J	K	L	M	N	O	P	Q	R	S	T	U	V	W	X	Y	Z
A	A	B	C	D	E	F	G	H	I	J	K	L	M	N	O	P	Q	R	S	T	U	V	W	X	Y	Z
B	B	C	D	E	F	G	H	I	J	K	L	M	N	O	P	Q	R	S	T	U	V	W	X	Y	Z	A
C	C	D	E	F	G	H	I	J	K	L	M	N	O	P	Q	R	S	T	U	V	W	X	Y	Z	A	B
D	D	E	F	G	H	I	J	K	L	M	N	O	P	Q	R	S	T	U	V	W	X	Y	Z	A	B	C
E	E	F	G	H	I	J	K	L	M	N	O	P	Q	R	S	T	U	V	W	X	Y	Z	A	B	C	D
F	F	G	H	I	J	K	L	M	N	O	P	Q	R	S	T	U	V	W	X	Y	Z	A	B	C	D	E
G	G	H	I	J	K	L	M	N	O	P	Q	R	S	T	U	V	W	X	Y	Z	A	B	C	D	E	F
H	H	I	J	K	L	M	N	O	P	Q	R	S	T	U	V	W	X	Y	Z	A	B	C	D	E	F	G
I	I	J	K	L	M	N	O	P	Q	R	S	T	U	V	W	X	Y	Z	A	B	C	D	E	F	G	H
J	J	K	L	M	N	O	P	Q	R	S	T	U	V	W	X	Y	Z	A	B	C	D	E	F	G	H	I
K	K	L	M	N	O	P	Q	R	S	T	U	V	W	X	Y	Z	A	B	C	D	E	F	G	H	I	J
L	L	M	N	O	P	Q	R	S	T	U	V	W	X	Y	Z	A	B	C	D	E	F	G	H	I	J	K
M	M	N	O	P	Q	R	S	T	U	V	W	X	Y	Z	A	B	C	D	E	F	G	H	I	J	K	L
N	N	O	P	Q	R	S	T	U	V	W	X	Y	Z	A	B	C	D	E	F	G	H	I	J	K	L	M
O	O	P	Q	R	S	T	U	V	W	X	Y	Z	A	B	C	D	E	F	G	H	I	J	K	L	M	N
P	P	Q	R	S	T	U	V	W	X	Y	Z	A	B	C	D	E	F	G	H	I	J	K	L	M	N	O
Q	Q	R	S	T	U	V	W	X	Y	Z	A	B	C	D	E	F	G	H	I	J	K	L	M	N	O	P
R	R	S	T	U	V	W	X	Y	Z	A	B	C	D	E	F	G	H	I	J	K	L	M	N	O	P	Q
S	S	T	U	V	W	X	Y	Z	A	B	C	D	E	F	G	H	I	J	K	L	M	N	O	P	Q	R
T	T	U	V	W	X	Y	Z	A	B	C	D	E	F	G	H	I	J	K	L	M	N	O	P	Q	R	S
U	U	V	W	X	Y	Z	A	B	C	D	E	F	G	H	I	J	K	L	M	N	O	P	Q	R	S	T
V	V	W	X	Y	Z	A	B	C	D	E	F	G	H	I	J	K	L	M	N	O	P	Q	R	S	T	U
W	W	X	Y	Z	A	B	C	D	E	F	G	H	I	J	K	L	M	N	O	P	Q	R	S	T	U	V
X	X	Y	Z	A	B	C	D	E	F	G	H	I	J	K	L	M	N	O	P	Q	R	S	T	U	V	W
Y	Y	Z	A	B	C	D	E	F	G	H	I	J	K	L	M	N	O	P	Q	R	S	T	U	V	W	X
Z	Z	A	B	C	D	E	F	G	H	I	J	K	L	M	N	O	P	Q	R	S	T	U	V	W	X	Y

'Let us continue our example. I shall use a ruler and write this out on the pad as we go along. Each letter of the keyword shows the particular line within the square to be used, so if the keyword was WATSON and the message was HELLOOLDCHAP, it is encrypted by cycling through the six lines where the first letters are W,A,T,S,O,N. So H = D in line W, E = E in line A, L = E in line T, L = D in line S, O = C in line O, O = B in line N, L = H in line W, D = D in line A, C = V in line T, H = Z in line S, A = O in line O, P = C in line N. The ciphertext becomes an apparently meaningless DEEDCBHDVZOC. To decrypt, the receiver reverses the process using the same keyword. Simple, isn't it, Watson?'

'Eh? Oh, yes. It's a complete doddle, Holmes. A piece of cake. Ah, at last.'

Lily entered the room like my personal saviour, carrying a tray that issued forth an array of aromas, sufficient to make any mouth water.

'Though' yer gen'lemen moight loike a spo' o' brekkie,' she said placing the tray on the table.

I needed no second bidding to tuck in, even though Holmes continued to babble on about codes and ciphers while we were eating.

'The sender and receiver could agree on a longer keyword, or the use of a key phrase to increase the complexity of the cipher. However, any polyalphabetic cipher has one inherent weakness, if a short key is used. It is the fact that the alphabets used for encryption are periodically repeated. That is what we must exploit, Watson. Watson?'

'Hhmm. This bacon is delicious, Holmes. You really must try it.'

No sooner had we finished breakfast than Holmes was back to the tedious French–sounding cipher, his energy re-doubled. I just wanted to snooze for a while.

'Now, Watson, the quickest way to break this code is to guess the keyword, using trial and error. We should know enough about our friend's childish mindset by now to do this successfully. Do try to stay awake, old chap, will you?'

'Whu ... oh, yes. Oh, indeed. I agree. Is there time for another pipe, perhaps?'

'No time. A man's life may depend upon the next few hours. Let us try the following sample keywords, to start with: SHERLOCK, HOLMES, HAMISH, WATSON,

MYCROFT, MORAN, PROFESSOR, MORIARTY, SEBASTIAN, RALPH, PARTRIDGE, DIOGENES, EDWARD, SIGER, FITZGERALD, MUSICAL, MURDER, IGNATIUS, DOYLE, CONAN, ARTHUR. I'll show you how to do it, and then we can split the work-load. We'll know very quickly whether something works or not, as the first few letters will make sense. If they don't, then we'll move on to the next one immediately.'

Holmes set about this seemingly impossible task with his customary zeal.

'Let us start by dividing the ciphertext into sets of five letters:

GFHKU EDIXH XPNZV LYRSP MPGVT VLA

Using SHERLOCK as a sample keyword, we must now move from the top row to the row of the key letters, cycling around the keyword again. First of all, G = Y in line S, F = M in line H, H = L in line E, K = B in line R, U = F in line L. I'll stop there, as my christian name is obviously *not* the keyword, the result being YMLBF, a meaningless combination of letters in the English language.'

'Zzzzzzzzzzzzzzz.'

'Watson! Wake up!'

'Eh? What? Where am I? Take that, you fuzzy-wuzzies! Oh, dear me, yes. Sorry, Holmes.'

'Now I shall have to repeat the lesson for you, using the keyword HOLMES.'

Believe it or not, I did manage to concentrate for long enough to understand how to translate the first 5 letters of the gobbledy-gook back into a different gobbledy-gook. At least, that is what happened to both of us over the following hour or so. Only when Holmes came to the keyword ARTHUR, did we make some form of progress. And he got very excited by it.

'We have it, Watson. We have it. Using ARTHUR as the keyword, the ciphertext
GFHKU EDIXH XPNZV LYRSP MPGVT VLA
translates into
GOODA NDREA DYNIC EEASY TIMET EST
So our clue to the fourth murder is:
GOODANDREADYNICEEASYTIMETEST
Or, 'Good and ready, nice easy time test.' What do you make of that clue, Watson?'

'Absolutely no sense whatsoever, apart from the keyword itself, which suggests that your theory of the childhood friend might be spot on. Is he playing games with us? It occurs to me, Holmes, that these murders must all have been planned well in advance, as otherwise how could the killer create all these complicated cipher-clues in the time between murders?'

'Good point. So they always planned to kill Ralph Partridge, even though he might not be musical.'

'Oo migh' no' be mewsical?'

'Oh, there you are, Lily. Never mind that. Come over here and see what you can make of this. It has us foxed completely.'

I was delighted that Holmes had considered asking Lily to examine our clue, but not half as delighted as she was. Instead of removing the breakfast tray, she sat down at the table, beaming, yet striving to look serious at the same time, as though she was about to sit an important examination.

'We are chasing a serial killer, Lily. He has already killed three people, each time leaving a clue. It usually tells us the name of the next victim. Here it is. *Good and ready, nice easy time test*. What does it mean?'

Holmes passed the piece of paper over to Lily, who sat gazing at it for about fifteen seconds. Then spoke.

'Dahn in the slave quawters, when oi'm no' busy cookin' for yer pair o' so-called flash 'arries, oi do moi crosswoids. The easies' clew is when oi gohha mayke a woid ouhha the foist lehhers of udder woids. Like G.A.R.N.E.T.T. Know anywun naimed Garnett? He's in a spohha bovver, ain't 'e?'

Smiling with pride, she handed the paper back to the two dumb-founded, so-called detectives.

Chapter XII

Bloomsbury.

Number 41 Gordon Square was a pleasant four-storey over basement Georgian terraced house, with window boxes on the first level, each filled to over-flowing with bright yellow primroses. Blinds were drawn to indicate a death in the white house. The square buzzed with a variety of motor cars, taxis and growlers. An odour of horse dung lay heavy in the air, a constant feature of London streets these days. The poor animals had never quite adjusted to the noise of their mechanised competitors.

We had travelled mercifully slowly through the London miasma in the same Beardmore that had taken us to the Diogenes Club. Holmes liked to use Ifan Rees as his regular cabbie, due to his enjoyment of the Welshman's occasional renditions of Gilbert and Sullivan operas:

'... your lordship would kindly reason with her and assure her officially that it is a standing rule at the Admiralty that love levels all ranks, her respect for an official utterance might induce her to look upon your offer in its proper light.
It is not unlikely. I will adopt your suggestion.
But soft, she is here.
Let us withdraw, and watch our opportunity.'

He had just finished singing *Things Are Seldom What They Seem* from *HMS Pinafore*, as we arrived at Gordon

Square and alighted from his taxi. I thought he was a rather good singer, for a cabbie. At least he had taken my mind off the journey itself.

After Lily's swift and rather embarrassing discovery of the meaning of our third clue, we quickly established the existence of several Garnetts in Holmes' indexes. A few of them were published authors, but only one was also a publisher. David Garnett ran a company called the Nonesuch Press and had recently published his novel – *A Man In The Zoo*. Did he have a connection to Bloomsbury? We hoped that James or Alix Strachey might throw some light on this subject, so that we could mount a guard over him and thereby catch our killer. Lestrade had been informed, and would supply backup when necessary. I had my Webley with me. Unpacking my bags would have to wait.

'Watson,' said Holmes, as we stood on the steps in front of number 41. 'We must tread softly here. We don't want to alarm anyone. It seems these murders are no longer about my family, which makes me begin to doubt the role of Conan Arthur in them. As being a musical man is a crime, it would perhaps be wise if we focused on the male friendships of both Partridge and this Garnett character, assuming they know him. We are here to examine the Partridge crime scene, and have also received a communication from someone who might be threatening the life of a person named David Garnett. That is all.'

'Right, Holmes. No mention whatsoever of music.'

'Mr. and Mrs Strachey are psychoanalysts, by the way. James studied under Sigmund Freud himself.'

‘Oh, good. They should be able to help us, then. It was obviously the mother.’ Good grief. Holmes was right. I *was* getting cranky in my old age.

The door was opened by a pretty young maid, who cringed visibly in the presence of the great detective, but gave me a cheeky smile behind his back as she took my coat. We were ushered into a drawing-room which was unexpectedly occupied by a group of eight men and three women. A couple of the men looked red-eyed, as though they had been crying. Many clutched hefty glasses of brandy or whisky. I supposed they had come to pay their respects. The atmosphere was subdued and reminded me of the airless staff room at the University Of London, full of pipe and cigarette smoke. The well-known economist John Maynard Keynes and the writer Virginia Woolf were the only faces I recognised through the haze, each puffing away vigorously on cheroots. There was silence when the maid announced ‘Mr. Sherlock Holmes and his friend, Dr. Watson’. Several pairs of eyes subjected us to what I might call *interested scrutiny*, for want of a better phrase. I did hope the word *friend* would not be misconstrued among this band of rabid libertarians.

‘Ah, Holmes. Most grateful to you for your concern over poor Ralph’s demise. It’s a real boon to us that you have come out of retirement. We are all most shocked by events. I am James Strachey.’

The speaker with the outstretched hand was a typical academic of the old school – late thirties, neatly-trimmed dark beard, plain c-bridge pince-nez, shabby tweed suit that had seen better days and the wettest of wet-fish handshakes. He looked like a nancy boy to me. To be honest, so did most of the men in the room. If I were to use Holmes' word – 'musical', then they could probably have formed a small chamber orchestra.

Holmes scanned the faces rapidly before concentrating on Mr. Strachey and replying.

'Not at all. I apologise for our intrusion. I would appreciate it if you could show me the room in which Mr. Partridge's body was found. Also I have a few questions to ask you, before I examine it.'

Holmes nodded to the glum, shocked entourage before following Strachey out of the room. 'Gentlemen. Ladies.'

Having no desire to be left alone amidst all those stares, I hurried after the pair down to the basement, which proved to be entirely empty, except for a huge raft of paintings and photographs that ranged across and against the four walls. Several of them were by some chap called Manet. They looked genuine enough, but there were far too many naked ladies in them for my taste. The room smelled of mice.

'First of all, Mr. Strachey,' said Holmes coldly. 'How did the murderer gain access to your house?'

'Good question. Neither the police nor I could find any sign of a break-in. The only logical conclusion is that poor Ralph let him in by the front door.'

'I see,' replied Holmes. 'So he probably knew Mr. Partridge. Secondly, do you know a Mr. David Garnett of the Nonesuch Press? The writer? Is he one of your ... group?'

'Bunny? Oh, yes, indeed. Everybody knows Bunny. But we are not a formal 'Group', Holmes. That is merely a media construct. We are a selection of close friends who share similar views on many subjects, both intellectual and artistic. There is no *movement*, as such.'

‘Can you tell me where Mr. Garnett is living? Where he might be now?’

‘Indeed. He lives with his wife Rachel in Hilton Hall. It’s near Huntingdon in Cambridgeshire. But most days he works in his bookshop, Birrell & Garnett at 19, Taviton Street, off the end of the square. He should be there now, if you want to find him. What’s this about, Holmes? I thought you were here to help find Ralph’s disgusting murderer.’

‘That is very true, Mr. Strachey,’ said Holmes. ‘Look, what I have to tell you must go no further than this room. Can I trust you?’

‘Most certainly. Of course I shall respect your confidence.’ James Strachey positively bridled at the thought that a public schoolboy and Cambridge graduate like him might be considered untrustworthy.

‘Good. Your friend Partridge is not the first victim of this killer. In fact he is the third, that we know of. And the first two were my own brother and father.’

‘Your father?’

‘Yes. Eh, we also received a communication from the killer that his next target would be someone called Garnett. We believe that he is a member of the Bloomsbury ... set.’

‘But why in God’s name is this lunatic killing people? Do you even know that?’

‘Not entirely. Although I have formed an opinion on it, I am not prepared to conjecture without more evidence. By any chance, do you happen to know if either Mr. Partridge or Mr. Garnett are members of the Diogenes Club, over in Pall Mall?’

At this question, James Strachey’s face turned a delicate shade of pink. He looked as though he was searching desperately for an acceptable lie that would enable him to avoid answering Holmes' question truthfully. Then his stiff upper lip ceased to tremble and he decided to give up altogether.

'Yes. Both of them. Actually, quite a few of our set are members there, and have been for some time. We value the peace and quiet it provides immensely. I knew your brother, Mycroft, you know? He used to attend our little soirées over here. His contributions were much appreciated for their wit and erudition. I was deeply saddened to hear that he had passed on. I had no idea his death had anything to do with Ralph.'

'Mycroft knew a lot of people. Mr. Strachey, I have no time to beat about the bush. Not only do we have the warning about Garnett, but we also have some evidence that the serial killer himself might come from within your bohemian set.'

If Holmes had intended to take the sting out of James Strachey's arrogant tail, he succeeded admirably. Strachey staggered slightly and leaned against the wall for support. But not for long. As became his class, he recovered quickly and was quite belligerent on the subject of Bloomsbury. Loyalty to the group was obviously high on his list of qualities.

'No. No. No. I refuse to believe such a thing, Holmes. You must be mistaken. Serial killers, indeed! We are the enlightened *Bloomsberries*, members of an *ancien régime*. Civilised life and friendship. We have no secrets from each other. Some of the best minds in the world are upstairs in this house. They are *geniuses*. Woolf, the great writer. Keynes, the great economist. Grant, the great painter. Do you understand? What exactly is this infernal evidence?'

I was fully prepared for the explosion that followed. There was nothing on this planet more inclined to resurrect Holmes' inner monster than the suggestion that other people were more intelligent than he. But I had no idea how deep the sword had gone. He was like a python in heat.

'Paper, Strachey. *Paper*,' spat Holmes. 'The exact same kind of unique paper that is used by the Hogarth Press to publish the drivelling nonsense that spouts from the mouths of your kin. That paper is being used to threaten my life. The life of Sherlock Holmes. And if you really wish a definition of the word *genius*, I suggest that you study the list of crimes that have been solved by Watson and myself in the past, and the criminals who have been brought to justice. Perhaps at the same time you might ask the question as to whether you and your band of troubadours would have been allowed to live the kind of lives that you are living without me. Now, leave. I wish to examine the scene of the crime. Go. Away.'

'What? How dare yo ...' spluttered Strachey.

'And do not mention this conversation to the mob upstairs. For all we know, the murderer may be sipping your brandy as we speak. We'll find our own way out, thank you.'

Strachey looked apoplectic. Like a dying fish, he opened his mouth to speak again, thought better of it, swivelled abruptly and left the room. Holmes strode over to the blood-stained wooden floor in the corner and proceeded to examine it carefully with his lens. I decided to keep out of his way until he had cooled down and wandered around the room looking at the paintings. *Tread softly*, my holy sainted grandmother.

After a while I plucked up enough courage to start humming to myself. The paintings seemed to be mainly portraits of men by other men, some of whose names I could identify from the photographs alongside them. I assumed both sitters and artists were members of the Bloomsbury set. Certainly Keynes was there. And Virginia Woolf. What extraordinary features she had! She looked like some kind of animal. A sheep. Not a wolf, of course. Goat? Yes. That was it. A goat. Names like Fry, Forster, Bell, Brenan meant nothing to me. Poor old Mycroft was in one of the group photographs, looking as sleepy as usual. He was lying on a blanket in someone's back garden on a bright, sunny day. It looked like a country house of some kind.

That was when I noticed the figure sitting on a bench behind him, and let out an almighty shriek of recognition.

'Holmes! Gosh, I'm sorry! Here! It's him! It's the same man! He's sitting behind Mycroft! Your brother!'

Holmes looked up impatiently from his business. 'What man, Watson?'

'The man from the library! Doyle! Ignatius bloody Doyle!'

Holmes rushed over to me and peered through his lens at the photograph of that rude bugger from the library while I continued to jab my finger at his image excitedly.

'Well?' I demanded. 'Is it him? Is this your childhood friend, Conan Arthur?'

'Steady on, Watson. It has been well over fifty years, you know.'

Holmes closely examined the face of the man sitting on the bench.

'Hhmm. It could be him. Poor chap. People do deteriorate in mental hospitals, you know. But the coincidence is too great. And there's nothing to be found here, except the footprints of a group of clumsy, clod-hopping policemen. I really must warn Lestrade to come to me first in future, before he involves the damn Yard. Look, I'll pursue this photograph with the spoilt left-wing intellectuals in the room of geniuses upstairs, if you hop around to that bookshop where Garnett works in Taviton Street. Call Lestrade along the way and ask him to have a constable mount guard on David Garnett. Wake him up if you have to. Wait for me there. I'll be over in half-an-hour. Then we might pay a visit to Mr. Ignatius Doyle at the British Museum.'

'Right, Holmes. I'm on my way.'

Frankly, I didn't know which was worse. The prospect of the staring room, or having to face Charity Pecksniff again.

Chapter XIII.

Kidnapped.

As things turned out, I didn't have to worry either way. The traumatic events of the next fifteen hours happened at such a speed that even now I have trouble separating one from another and applying an accurate timeline. I do remember stepping out onto Gordon Square and turning in the direction of Taviton Street. Although it was a short walk, because of the density of fog I decided to respond to Mr Rees' questioning nod as he polished his pet Beardmore taxi-cab. I felt a little sorry for him, waiting outside for another fare, and mistook his continued presence for loyalty to Sherlock Holmes. I also thought to enjoy another short stretch of Gilbert & Sullivan on my journey. But it was surely the biggest mistake of my life.

'19, Taviton Street, cabbie,' I announced cheerily as I clambered aboard. 'On With The Motley! I have a preference for 'The Mikado', by the way!'

'Four-fifths a king and one-fifth a God,' muttered the Welshman as he climbed behind the wheel.

I settled myself into the seat and prepared for Ifan Rees' solo performance as we pulled into the road. Sure enough:

'As some day it may happen that a victim must be found,
I've got a little list – I've got a little list
Of society offenders who might well be underground,
And who never would be missed – who never would be missed!

There's the pestilential nuisances who write for autographs,
All people who have flabby hands and irritating laughs,
All children who are up in dates, and floor you with 'em flat,
And all third persons who on spoiling tête-á-têtes insist,
They'd none of 'em be missed — they'd none of 'em be missed!'

We had reached the far side of Gordon Square and were moving slowly into Taviton Street behind a growler when the door of the cab flew open and in climbed, to my horror and annoyance, that appalling weedy character from the British Museum, Ignatius Doyle, complete with feathery goatee and vicious grin.

'How dare you, sir?' I shouted. 'This is my cab! Get out of here immediately or I shall call the police!'

His response was to giggle manically and grab me roughly by the neck with his left hand while applying some kind of sweet-smelling pad to my face with his right. I struggled for my Webley but became confused as to its location in the heat of the moment. Then I began to lose consciousness, a single word floating through my head – chloroform, chloroform, chlorof ....

I awoke in darkness, not knowing what had happened or where I was. I had to wait a while for my eyes to focus and adjust to a faint yellow light emanating from a crack beneath a wide doorway in front of me. My mouth felt as dry as a desert and sharp pains shot down from my shoulders and hands to my legs. I tried to move, but could not. That was when I realised I had been shackled to a concrete wall, like Jesus Christ in the crucifixion position. My toes barely touched the ground, which was stained red in a rough semi-circle. Looking around, I saw that I was in some sort of garage, containing a single Beardmore taxi-cab. Suddenly remembering the crimes that Holmes and I were investigating, I was relieved to establish that I was still fully clothed. Stupidly, my first reaction was one of hunger. I hadn't had any lunch. My stomach grumbled noisily. I must have been strung up for several hours. When would I eat again? If ever? Who had kidnapped me? Was Ignatius Doyle actually Conan Arthur, Sherlock's childhood friend? What was he doing in that weird Welsh singer's cab? I pushed and pulled against the shackles but only managed to achieve fresh spikes of torment. My groans gave me the idea of shouting for help, which I did with some gusto.

'Helpm! Someonem! I'vem beenm kidnappedm bym pervertedm, murderousm serialm killersm! They'rem killingm musicalm menm!'

The muffled words echoed inside my head, and it was only then that I understood I had been gagged as well as bound. With some bandage smelling of antiseptic that almost made my gorge rise. Gagged like Mycroft and Edward Holmes. Great Heavens! Oh, yes, I had reached my three score and ten and would not have been too unhappy to join my parents and my two wives on the right hand side of God the Father Almighty. But not that way! Sweet Jesus! Not by emasculation!

Suddenly I heard a bolt being drawn back and the huge door slid across to show two figures outlined against a dim, old-fashioned street gas lamp, onc tall and thin, one very short and tubby. A light clicked on, causing me to blink.

‘Go ahead. Shout as much as you like. Nobody can hear your muffled grunts.’

The speaker was the odious Doyle, who crunched his way over towards me through some dry leaves and stood, breathing his fetid garlic breath into my face, followed by Ifan Rees, whose bald head reflected the light from a bare bulb overhead. A freezing fog had followed them through the door. I determined to behave as though I could speak clearly.

‘Holmesm willm bem herem soonm, mym friendsm. Andm thenm them pairm ofm youm willm getm them soundm whippingm youm deservem. Followedm bym am specialm punishmentm thatm hem hasm linedm upm form youm.’

The pair laughed at my muzzled words. Then the silly dwarf Rees started to dance around the garage and sing again:

‘Behold the Lord High Executioner
A personage of noble rank and title –
A dignified and potent officer,
Whose functions are particularly vital!
Defer, defer,
To the Lord High Executioner!
Defer, defer,
To the noble Lord, to the noble Lord,
To the Lord High Executioner!’

‘Be quiet, Ifan. Yes, I do hope the world’s first consulting detective comes to your rescue,’ said Doyle, his face white with anger. ‘That is actually the plan, Watson, *old fellow*. Youm arem them baitm. Then the interfering meddler can suffer the same fate as his brother and father and all of the other goats. Followed by you. Ifan has his farmer's weapon handy, don't you, Ifan?'

At this prompt, the baby-faced lunatic whipped out an evil-looking blood-stained slaughter knife and held it against my throat.

'Getm awaym, youm baldm lunaticm! Andm youm won'tm getm Davidm Garnettm, youm knowm! He'sm beingm guardedm bym them policem.'

More muffled sounds.

Doyle's manner changed abruptly. He turned to his Welsh side-kick and shoved him back by the shoulder. Rees backed away from him.

'I told you that last so-called *clue* was much too simple, you bloody nincompoop. Holmes was bound to break your silly, childish ciphers at some stage. We could have done the whole business much better without them. Now we shall have to change our plans.'

'Aw, but granddad. Iggy. It took them long enough to get that one, eh? We're as smart as them two geriatrics. And it doesn't matter anyway. To hell with this Garnett character. The next clue'll bring old Sherlock right to us, assuming he can break it. Then you can have your revenge at last. That's what the others were about, weren't they? Getting back at the great detective?'

'Maybe. Maybe not. What do you know about my motives? Just deliver whatever clue you've devised for Holmes right now to 221B Baker Street. Include Partridge's meat and two veg in the package. That should focus his mind. All right. Go on. Take the cab and be quick about it. I'll stay here and have a little chat with Snowy. Tell him some home truths about his great friend, Sherlock Holmes.'

'Snowym? Whom arem youm callingm Snowym? Howm darem youm?'

My stifled complaint only led to more hoots of laughter from them both.

Chapter XIV.

Conan Arthur.

'I apologise for my half-educated grandson's behaviour, Snowy. He is young at the game of life as yet. I rather fear that my daughter made a significant mistake in marrying a mere Welshman, rather than a Yorkshireman. There may be some ... simplicity there. I taught him some basic mathematics and literature and it went to his hairless little head. His knowledge of ciphers is skimpy, to say the least. But he is surely handy with a butcher's knife. And Gilbert & Sullivan, of course. Not so handy with a gun, fortunately. It was his decision to take a pot shot at Holmes in The Stranger's Room, not mine. I had to have words with him about that. He came close to depriving me of my final piece of performance art.'

Doyle reclined his bony skeleton upon an oil canister and lit a strange-looking cigarette. He blew smoke up towards the ceiling through the corner of his mouth and narrowed his piggy eyes. That was when I realised he was smoking marijuana, as I believe it is called nowadays.

'I wonder how well you know your glorious colleague, Dr Watson? How well you know the real William Sherlock Scott Holmes, the great detective? He of the hooded, chiselled features and the furrowed, intellectual brow? The violinist, cocaine addict and chemistry playboy? Not at all, I suspect. I knew him as a boy when we played together in the fields near Hillcroft

House in Yorkshire. That was a long time ago. A lifetime.'

My captor paused, in what I imagined was an attempt to look tragic.

'My lifetime, actually. The real name's Conan Arthur, by the way. I adopted the other name after my first stint in the snake pit. Changed my accent, too. Nobody was going to know anything about my past life. I was turning over a new leaf, a new page in the book, if you like.'

Doyle jumped off the canister and started to walk around the garage. I continued my attempts to slide one hand through a shackle. And listened.

'He was a very good sportsman in those days, your friend. There was a time when we discussed the chance of a career for him in county cricket – I was nowhere near as good – but his interest in ball sports waned later on, to be replaced by his private little scientific world and some wierdo Japanese fighting nonsense. As you see, I have been following very closely the exploits of the Bobbsey Twins in The Strand Magazine. I know a lot more about your lives than you might imagine. Hah! Dozens and dozens of years spent stalking the pair of you, and never once caught! One evening I plucked up enough courage to pass by the pair of you in Baker Street and mutter, "Good Evening, Sherlock Holmes". And you thought it was Irene Adler in disguise! Then there was the occasion, during what you subsequently called your investigation of The Solitary Cyclist, that I imagined Holmes recognised me in some pub I'd followed him to in the country. He'd got involved in a boxing match and done rather well. I was almost proud of him. All this was after I got out of Bethlem, of course.

Deemed to be mended, I was, and fit for re-entering the community. Hee-hee-hee. Oh, hah! Hah! Wheee!'

At this, Doyle went into a fit of giggles, which only came to a halt when he had a coughing seizure. It took him a while to recover. The rattling within his chest gave me the pleasurable hope that he might be seriously ill. Not that it mattered, if he was intent on bringing Holmes down with him. I struggled yet again with my ropes, but to no avail. Strangely, hanging from a wall seemed to ease the pain from my old war wound.

'Don't bother, *old fellow*. You are bound with those ropes until the next stage of our plan. The final solution, you might call it. You should really hope that Holmes can't crack our last cipher and clue to get here, as that is when you will both meet your Maker. Now where was I? Oh, yes. The true story of the childhood of Sherlock Holmes. I don't know what he has told you about that subject, but prepare yourself for a shock, Watson. The humble, loyal and faithful servant. I bet he didn't tell you that we were lovers, did he?'

Again I pushed and pulled to contradict his filthy lies. Doyle ignored me. He seemed to lose himself in some fantasy world of the past.

'We were teenagers, and I was living in a cabin out in the Carperby woods around Richmond. I'd run away from home, actually. My parents couldn't stand my feminine traits and the idea of their son being a bundle of sticks, a *faggot* who liked dressing up in his mother's clothes. A *homosexual*. What a nasty word that is. Not half as acceptable as the word *heterosexual*, eh, Snowy? But not for broad-minded Sherlock. Handsome, intellectual, beautiful Sherlock. He was hungry for all the experiences that life could offer him in those days.'

Doyle stood in front of me again, and gazed into my eyes, as though to emphasize the point he was making.

'Yes, we were lovers,' he said dreamily. 'Young lovers for all of two weeks. Every night we experimented with ways of expressing our feelings for each other. It was his first, innocent experience of the perils of the flesh.'

Doyle threw away his cigarette and returned to sit on the canister.

'That is to say, *I* was in love with *him*. In exactly the same way that you were in love with each of your two wives, Snowy. Both of whom you have lost, so I would expect you to know how I felt then. Sherlock? Apparently he was merely in *lust* with me. Not the same thing, I think you'll agree. Then it was all over. He told me that he wasn't *cut out* – his very words – for that sort of thing, that he was too conventional and didn't want to end up in *queer* street. He left me in my cabin to my own devices. Walked away one day without a backward glance. My God! I had never imagined that such exquisite pain could exist! It turned my mind to sawdust. I stopped eating - there wasn't that much anyway, without his contributions, apart from berries – and sleeping. I'd wander the woods at night, baying like a wolf at the moon. I didn't care about anything. Whether I lived or died was immaterial to me. I stopped washing and defecated and pissed anywhere and everywhere. All I wanted was Sherlock back in my arms at night and his lips upon mine.'

I heaved away at those cursed ropes to take my mind off what that damned rotten liar was saying. Holmes kissing another man! The very idea!

'Things came to a head one evening. I shall never forget it. I decided to approach his house to plead with him to take me back. He met me at the gate, enraged that I should attempt to *destroy his life* – his actual words, Snowy. We came to blows and he hurt me badly, being a much better boxer than myself. I limped back into the forest and my cabin and lay there for about a week without moving an inch. Then the treacherous bastard decided that my presence even in the woods was too much of a risk to his precious future, and sent for the whitecoats. That was in ... let me see – 1872. Do you know how many years I spent in bedlam, Snowy? No? Twenty. Two zero. Twen-tee! Over a quarter of my life shoved down the toilet by that devious charlatan. The subsequent incarcerations were also due to him, in my opinion, although he was by then a famous personality and I just a little-known librarian. With a deadly secret in his heart, admittedly. One that I could never announce, because ... because I *still* love him, even now. Can you understand that?'

I gave up struggling and tried to stand on the ground as much as I could with my good leg, to soften the excruciating pain in my lower back. But I could not bring myself to look into the eyes of this madman.

'Of course you can't. I wouldn't expect you to.'

Suddenly Doyle doubled over and fell off the canister. He lay groaning on the ground for a full minute, and then twisted around to vomit profusely onto some leaves on the floor. His face reached a shade of puce. He retched again and again. Then he took something out of a pocket and swallowed it. After a short while he recovered slightly and stood up, rubbing his stomach.

'Sorry about that, *old fellow*. Just a spot of stomach cancer. Nothing to worry about. Not after a few more months, anyway. That's all I've got left. You might wonder why am I bothering to extract my vengeance on the goats at this late stage? And why those particular goats? Well, here's one you'll remember: *Vengeance is mine, sayeth the Lord*, and all that. When you get the old come-hither, that's the time to settle scores. With the people who destroyed MY life!'

Doyle had turned around to me and screamed the word in my face with his foul breath. Those piggy eyes were popping out of his head. The goatee shone with spittle and he stank to high heaven. His body was obviously rotting away. The man's reason hung by a slender thread and he looked like he should be back in Bethlem at that very moment. In a straitjacket.

'Yes. Perhaps you'd be interested in knowing how these people destroyed my life, Snowy. I observed your career with Sherlock closely and I have come to the conclusion that you are a decent, loyal, straightforward human being, in a world of deviants. One righteous man in sorrow, as my old man used to say, before he stopped talking to me. I may even let you live after I punish Sherlock, so that you can immortalise me in print. What shall we call it? *Sherlock Holmes And The Vengeance Of Conan Arthur*? Sounds good to me.'

He had calmed down and returned to his canister.

'There was always a plan. I spent my entire adult life outside hospital, constructing an appropriate revenge for all those people who had taken love from me and promised love in return, without delivering. And there are so many! Can you imagine what happens to a person like me in a mental hospital, Snowy? The vicious lunatics who attacked me every night and left me bleeding and half-dead? They used me as a pin cushion. Twenty years of it. I can't get back at them now, as most of them are either dead or still incarcerated. But the others. Well.'

Doyle folded his hands around his knees, leaned back and stared into space.

'Mycroft wasn't the first, you know? Oh, the others will never be found, I can assure you. I was on my own then, without any of Ifan's silly ciphers or the knife stuff. I was strong enough to strangle them and lose their bodies in the Thames, with a cement necklace. You wouldn't know them, but they were guilty of the same crime. Pretending to love Conan Arthur. Using me for their own pleasure, and then dumping me. Now you're probably asking yourself: Why Mycroft? Why old man Holmes? Why Partridge and Garnett? Why the Bloomsbury Group, who were so good to me after Mrs Woolf helped me to recover from my illness and introduced me to their wonderful world of literature, politics and art, a world that I had never known before?'

The lunatic was silent for a moment. He wet his lips with a snake-like tongue.

'When I was that teenager, before I fell in love with Sherlock, I had been introduced to the world of sex by Sherlock's father, old Mr. Holmes himself. I was thirteen then and had no idea what was happening to me. Totally ignorant, I was. He forced himself upon me one day in the hay barn. He was just a smelly old drunk and I was disgusted and felt filthy afterwards, but at the same time, I knew that if he had treated me differently ...? Well. He must have talked to his eldest son about me, as he started in on me as well. That was when I began to wax clever and demanded payment from them each time.'

I was struggling to close my ears to this horrifying story, but failing badly. I noticed the murderous rat had started to cry.

'Needless to say, Sherlock knew nothing about me and his father and brother. I didn't want him to, as I valued what we had together so much. I don't know if they ever told him, or if he worked it out for himself. He is the great brain, after all. And so I gained my just revenge on Edward Holmes. He even provided lunch for us that day, he was so pleased to see me, and to meet my grandson, who sang him one of his witty ditties. Little did he know what we had in mind for him. Then it was clever little Ifan's idea that I straddle the wheelchair, so there'd only be one set of footprints on the way to the barn. And a piggy-back on returning to the kitchen. Another puzzle for Sherlock! Mycroft was even easier, as I am a member of the Diogenes Club, and all we had to do was wait for him to fall asleep in his chair, and for everyone else to leave. As for Partridge ... well, same, same really. Although we were interrupted before we had finished with him by the return of Strachey and his ugly wife, and had to make a hurried exit out the back door. Hah! Good old Ralph enjoyed his bread buttered on both sides. Man or woman, he didn't mind which.'

Doyle pulled his sleeve across his eyes to wipe away his tears.

'And now it seems there's one goat left, the only person I ever really loved, who abandoned me at a critical time in my life, and who was responsible for everything that came afterwards – all those years in and out of mental hospitals. I can't describe to you what that was like. You would have to experience it for yourself. Mrs Woolf rescued me, right enough, and I'll always be grateful to her. She gave me copies of her books to read, but I couldn't make sense of them. And I couldn't keep up with that Bloomsbury set, no matter how hard I tried. They seemed to know everything about everything. I was lost inside the group, and had to get out as soon as I could. For the sake of my own self-esteem, if for no other reason. Meeting Mycroft again was fun, though. He pretended not to remember me, but I knew that he did. So I made a point of staying close to him, and making myself available to him, if you know what I mean? He didn't respond, being so far up the chain of government by then that being seen with a dirtbag like me might damage his career. I embarrassed him. Hah! Do you know why I call myself the Goatslayer, Snowy? Because goats butt each other. And they are fastidious about cleanliness and they like a frequent change of feed. That's why. Oh, Holy Mother Of God! Sweet Jesus!'

Doyle had fallen off the canister onto the floor and lay clutching his stomach in agony. He struggled to get something from a pocket and put it into his mouth. Some sort of morphine tablet, I assumed. I found myself hoping that he might not die just yet, and leave me in the hands of his lunatic knife-wielding grandson. But the pill did its work and he recovered.

'I need to get some stronger painkillers. Why the religious quote, I hear you ask, Snowy? My poor darling Ifan, a child of Sodom if ever there was one, is actually quite a believer. A good Catholic. Like all musical men, he feels that his true nature is an abberation and that Jude, bond-servant of Jesus Christ and brother to James the less, was right when he wrote those words. We are truly a group of unfortunates who are filled with self-loathing and a destiny of eternal fire is what we yearn for. So he thinks, anyway. I'm not that bothered any more. Heaven or hell, I'll take either. But Sherlock will go before me, and who knows what his destiny will be, eh? Up or down?'

Doyle swivelled his thumb upwards and downwards. Giggling, he turned on his heel abruptly and walked towards the garage door.

'So long, Snowy. Until tomorrow, anyway. Holmes won't be here to rescue you before then. And Ifan and I are going to a party tonight. My last ever musical occasion. Wish me luck. Nighty night.'

'Youm can'tm leavem mem herem likem thism,' I choked. 'Youm madm swinem! Helpm! Helpm!'

Chapter XV.

The Fourth Puzzle.

To continue my narrative, it is necessary for me to document the events that occurred to Sherlock Holmes during the same period, and which he told me about later on, after he had rescued me from a fate worse than death. It was in the early hours of the following morning, and we were sitting in front of a roaring fire at 221B Baker Street following a quite stupendous feast of Lily's, smoking our post-prandial pipes. Lestrade had departed with relief to his bed. I envied him heartily, being exhausted and full of aches and pains from the experience of hanging on a wall like Jesus Christ for over fifteen hours. But I needed to know what had happened from Holmes' side of the story. And, hand on heart, I must admit that I did actually fall asleep for a few of those vertical hours.

'When I returned to the room of genius with the photograph, it was Mrs Woolf who confirmed that Ignatius Doyle had been a member of their group for a while, some time ago. The picture had been taken in Berkshire, where the Carrington woman was living with Partridge and James Strachey's elder brother, Lytton.'

'The *menage a trois*. Oh, I do remember.'

'Then as I was leaving, a subdued James Strachey – I think he was trying to mend the fences between us – told me confidentially that Virginia Woolf had met Ignatius Doyle for the first time when they were fellow patients in a psychiatric hospital called Bethlem in St George's Fields, Southwark. She took an interest in his welfare and they became friendly. She introduced him to the Bloomsbury Group after his illness and lent him some of her books. That was when I knew for certain that Ignatius Doyle must be my childhood friend, Conan Arthur. And it confirmed my suspicion that he had to be involved in these murders. Ralph Partridge would have known him. The threads were beginning to weave a pattern.'

'So you didn't go to the British Museum after all?' I asked. In my heart I knew that I was never going to be able to quiz Holmes about that teenage affair with Conan Arthur. It might destroy our relationship forever, and I did not want that. I had to accept the possibility that it might have happened and he would never admit to it. But what did I understand about the physical attraction between man and man? Absolutely nothing. After all, he had been a veritable child, and probably didn't know what he was doing.

'No. I rang the British Museum from the bookshop to see if he was at work, which he obviously was not. They had no home address for him. It seems that he was a bit of an itinerant. Anyway, I already had my suspicions as to where I might find Mr. Doyle later that night, thanks to Scotland Yard. I waited for you in the bookshop for over an hour, and began to get worried for your safety, Watson. I called young Lestrade myself and he arrived directly from his visit to Virginia Woolf's house in Tavistock Square, where he informed Leonard Woolf, her husband, of the neighbour's complaints about noise and, more importantly, of the Hogarth Press paper link with the murders. Woolf became very compliant, as he was most concerned for his wife's well-being – apparently an ongoing problem for him – and informed

Lestrade in confidence about a secret club for musical men that existed in London, where they could get together and socialise. He didn't know where it was, but said it was simply called Pyotr's Cave, after the composer Tchaikovsky. And apparently there is to be a big party tonight.'

'I suppose you're going to tell me now that Tchaikovsky was also a musical man?' I enquired grumpily.

'Yes, Watson. Actually he was. In more ways than one. But he got married for the sake of the family name, as many musical men did in those days. And still do, of course. A deeply unhappy and tormented personal life seems to be the destiny of such men and women. But not forever, I hope. The marriage lasted two and one half months, which just about beats Edward Fitzgerald's record, I suppose. We explained the danger to a very reluctant David Garnett, who had to be persuaded to accept a police guard. Like his cohorts in the Bloomsbury Group, I believe he thought he was above such bourgois considerations as personal safety.'

Holmes paused to relight his pipe before continuing.

'But then he had never been tested, had he? Not like you, old boy. First in Afghanistan and then so many times afterwards with me down the years, and now this latest challenge. Every examination passed with flying colours. What would I do without you, Watson?'

He leaned across and squeezed my arm fondly.

'How did you work it all out, Holmes?' I asked. I was in no mood for nostalgia, or any of his magic trickery, where he would play his games with the truth before pulling the solution out of a hat for the benefit of an idolising client. It was one of my companion's most annoying traits. I was too physically and mentally exhausted and just wanted to test my new bed.

'It is true, Watson, that I had an intuition about these crimes from an early stage, because of that childhood friendship going rotten. Yet I failed to perceive the common denominator to each of the victims for some time. Once Partridge was killed, and Garnett threatened, it occurred to me that it had to be our old friend, the Diogenes Club. I questioned Garnett about Pyotr's Cave and where it was. He swore blind that he had never heard of such a place, and wouldn't be caught dead in one anyway, as he was a happily married man. But I knew he was lying. It's the eyes that betray guilt, Watson. Lestrade seemed quite shocked even to think that it existed. So I decided to return to number 221B Baker Street and contemplate my twin problems over a pipe or two: what had happened to you, and the location of Pyotr's Cave. I felt that the answer to one might provide me with the answer to the other.

Holmes blew smoke rings to the ceiling with obvious pleasure as he appeared to collect his thoughts.

'I was making very little progress and well into my second pipe when Lily appeared with a package, saying that it had just been pushed through the letterbox. Inside were the genital remains of Ralph Partridge, and an envelope. I rushed to the window to see if I could recognise anyone on the street. Sure enough, Ifan Rees was there, polishing his taxi-cab as usual. But at the time I had no idea of his relationship to Conan Arthur. I placed the package on the mantel for Lestrade and checked the envelope. Inside it was yet another clue, presumably telling me the identity of the next victim. Here it is.'

Holmes handed me a piece of the same paper that had been used in each of the other clues, folded over again. It was more of the same gobbledegook.

Even as Sodom and Gomorrah, and the cities about them in like manner, giving themselves over to fornication, and going after strange flesh, are set forth for an example, suffering the vengeance of eternal fire.
Think on your sins, Sherlock Holmes, as you are on the list:
4. 'hhkroyrqlqqurwccupslmdrnhk'.
Love and bubbles, The Goatslayer.

I was in no mood for breaking codes, so I passed it back to him and asked him to explain it in words of one syllable, if possible.

'Of course, old man. You must be exhausted. Once she had recovered from seeing Partridge's bits and pieces, I invited Lily to assist me in my deliberations and was pleasantly surprised again at her quick-wittedness. You were right about our housekeeper, Watson. She is a bright spark. We really must make more use of her in the future. It took us all of two hours to work out the solution to the fourth cipher. I guessed that our cryptographer friend would not use the same cipher method as before, as he would want to impress me, so it came down to either an Atbash, ADFGVX or a Playfair. Don't worry, the explanation isn't that complex. A swift check proved that it wasn't an Atbash, where the letters of the alphabet are simply reversed, and Z=A, Y=B, etc., One of the clues to a Playfair cipher is the absence of the letter J in the ciphertext, which was indeed the case with our one, and so I plumped for a

Playfair. Lily and I used a similar trial and error approach with the different keys that you and I did on the previous cipher. This time I tried ARTHUR and CONAN first, with no luck. But our third guess of the key was SHERLOCK, and it worked.'

'You had better explain how this Playfair cipher operates, Holmes, before you go any further. I'm a bit lost.' Lost, and struggling to keep my eyes open.

'Of course. It was invented by Sir Charles Wheatstone in 1854. He named it after his friend, Lyon, the first Baron Playfair of St Andrews, who promoted its use in the field, specifically the Boer and Great Wars. I'll write it out for you, using our previous example of HELLOLDCHAP. The Playfair cipher functions by replacing each pair of letters, or digraph, in the plaintext with a different pair. To encrypt, the key is first placed at the head of the remaining letters of the alphabet within a 5 by 5 square (although other shapes can be used), as follows:

S	H	E	R	L
O	C	K	A	B
D	F	G	I/J	M
N	P	Q	T	U
V	W	X	Y	Z

Looking at the Playfair square, if both letters of a digraph are in the same row, they are replaced by the letters right beside them (wrapping around at the end); if they fall in the same column, by the letters beneath them (ditto); if diagonal, each letter is replaced with the letter in the same row, but the other letter's column. So our plaintext of

HE-LL-OO-LD-CH-AP
becomes the ciphertext
ER-SS-DD-SM-FC-CT
and the recipient can decrypt it by simply reversing the rules. Because he knows the key. Anyone who intercepts the message cannot break it without that key. Here you are. Simple, isn't it?'

Holmes handed me his workings. I understood broadly what he was saying, and glanced at it briefly, before handing it back. The sooner he finished talking, the sooner I could get to my bed.

'Oh, a mere bagatelle. So what did our plaintext become when you reversed the Playfair ciphertext?' I asked knowledgeably.

'It became: SSAEAVETEUPTHYOOTNLRIMSTEC. I was a bit flummoxed by this, but again Lily came up trumps. It was a very simple clue, she said. All that was required was to create new words from every third letter, cycling around the clue. She'd done this many times down in the slave quarters. Sure enough, this produced: SEEUHOLMESATPYTRSCAVETONIT. *See you, Holmes, at Pyotr's Cave tonight*. The spelling foxed us for a while, but I decided it must have been written by a semi-literate person, possibly a sidekick of Doyle's. I was obviously the next victim, and I suppose I knew that was coming. But where on earth was Pyotr's Cave? Then I remembered the first rule of detection: *when you have eliminated the impossible, whatever remains, however improbable, must be the truth.*'

I smiled at the old cliché. How many times in the past had it proved correct? Countless.

Holmes continued his soliloquy, amid my frequent yawns.

‘When we examined the Diogenes Club, Watson, we focused on the building itself, and the rooms therein. But we forgot about the *garden* at the back. And the twin garages. What if Pyotr’s Cave was entered from the rear of the building through the garden and into some sort of underground tunnel? Or from one of the garages? That was when I had my divine inspiration. I would disguise myself as a musical man and try to infiltrate this private club, with the help of Jasper Lestrade. That is why you see me dressed like this now.’

‘I did wonder at your strange get-up,’ I replied dryly. ‘You look like an aging actor who has just finished a production of Oscar Wilde’s *The Importance Of Being Earnest*, and forgotten to remove his make-up.’

‘Yes, I know, but it was necessary, old chap. If I could imitate a woman, I could surely dress up as one of your nancy-boys, complete with cravat, silk shirt, cigarette-holder, tight trousers, Cuban heels, delicate moustache, a bit of a lisp. And malacca stick sword, of course. Although he complained a bit about lack of sleep, Lestrade was surprisingly keen on exploring his feminine side. That made me wonder a bit, but I did need him as backup, so to speak. Lily enjoyed helping us make ourselves up, even using some lipstick on Jasper, with whom she was beginning to get on like a house on fire. He looked quite like a young Tchaikovsky, with his pasted-on beard. She wanted to disguise herself as a man and join us, but I had to put my foot down on that idea. After all, I was going to meet the serial killer himself, if my guess about the Diogenes Club was accurate. Danger beckoned. So off we pranced, Watson. In a growler, you’ll be glad to know. There were no hackneys about, for some reason.’

‘What time was this?’ I asked. Lily and Jasper? House on fire?

‘About ten o’clock last night.’

Chapter XVI.

Pyotr's Cave.

'It was ten-fifteen when our Clarence pulled up, clippety-clop, clippety-clop, at the rear of the Diogenes Club on Carlton House Terrace. During the trip I had updated Lestrade with the story of my childhood friend, Conan Arthur, and his difficult life. When I told him of my suspicion that he was the killer of the musical men, he smiled grimly and patted the British Bulldog Webley in his jacket pocket. I found myself wishing that his father had been his equal in strength, intelligence and character. We might have solved many more cases and relieved the British taxpayer of the cost of quite a few trials and life sentences.'

'That's vigilante talk, Holmes,' I put in tiredly.

'Of course it is, Watson. Our time together has been just that. A vigil against crime. But we are running out of years, and I have observed many recent cases where the legal process seems to favour the criminal rather more than the victim. I intend to redress the balance to the best of my ability during the rest of my life. With your assistance, of course.'

'Holmes!'

'To continue. The pair of delicate nancy-boys alighted stylishly from the growler and gazed through the dense, dripping fog at the sinister twin garage fronts for a possible entrance to Pyotr's Cave. But all was as silent as the grave. We could not even hear the traffic in Pall Mall. Like Ali Baba, I willed some jinn to arrive and for a magical door to open, *sesame*-like. And after a few minutes, it worked. Not a jinn, exactly, but the Diogenes doorkeeper Joseph, who emerged from within the hedgerow like a wraith, lost in the dark of the night. His pale features and plaited blonde hair gleamed beneath the dim gas lighting. A pair of black round eyes finally stopped moving and stared into mine with deep suspicion. Yet I don't believe the innocent child recognised either one of us.'

' "Password?" he asked.'

'I had not anticipated this problem and was forced to think quickly. What kind of password would a club like this use? I decided that it must be something to do with Tchaikovsky's music. A rapid mental flicking provided Swan, Lake, Sleeping, Beauty, Romeo, Juliet, Pathetic, Nutcracker ...'.

' "Nutcracker," I replied with absolute confidence. There was a flash of white teeth from the simple-minded pickaninny as he beckoned us to follow him into the hedge, which proved to be merely a few branches at the end of a garden. Joseph disappeared through a small wicket gate at the side of the first garage, and we bent down to follow him into what appeared to be a large padded cell, whose walls were lined with thick beige cushions. Watson, if I had only known that you were in crucifixion mode next door, I would surely have rushed to your rescue then and there. You do believe me, don't you?'

'Oh, of course, Holmes. Of course. That explains why I could not hear anyone coming or going through it. Eh, what exactly *was* in the other garage, as a matter of interest?'

'Nothing. Except for a dirty rolled-up loop of carpet and a metal trapdoor in the middle of the floor. It was evidently quite heavy, as Joseph had to use both hands to lift it up, revealing a flickering light and a set of steps leading down to ... what? Dante's Inferno? Perhaps. Music drifted up from below. Grinning, he invited us to enter the dungeon. I clasped my stick sword firmly and stepped forward, followed closely by Lestrade. Our descent was steep and led to the middle of a candle-lit tunnel hewn out of pure granite stone. A bright crimson arrow had been stencilled onto the wall, pointing towards the left. We followed it dutifully. Rose petals were strewn along the floor and colourful balloons hung from the roof. There was an unusually sweet smell that I recognised later as incense, burnt to hide the odour of cannibis resin. It became much warmer and sweat began to sting my eyes. The music grew louder as we progressed along the twisting corridor for several minutes, passing other arrows at forks in the shadowy passage. Wherever we were going, it could not have been anywhere near the Diogenes Club. By my judgement, if we were heading for Pyotr's Cave, it was probably underneath the Carlton Club. Then I remembered that certain private clubs in London had built underground shelters for their members during the Great War, in case of bombing from Count Zeppelin's airships. They were dotted around the city, and some of them could still be functional.'

' "What is that awful sentimental music?" whispered Lestrade.'

' "That, young Jasper, son of the late Inspector George, is the *Rose Adagio* from Pyotr Ilyich Tchaikovsky's *Sleeping Beauty Suite* for the ballet," I replied somewhat testily. "And it is one of the most beautiful pieces of music ever composed by man or beast." '

' "Oh, I believe you," the youthful philistine muttered in reply.'

'We had come to the end of the passage and were staring at a completely blank rockface. The music emanated from the other side at full volume, together with a low buzzing sound, like that from a hive of bees, servicing their queen. It had got quite clammy and we were both bathed in perspiration. I searched the wall in vain to find some key. Then Lestrade pointed at the floor, where a tiny button was sticking up, like a skittle waiting to be knocked down. Or a land mine? I stood on it tentatively, and the wall vanished miraculously into the roof with a soft *whoosh*, like a lift travelling upwards. We edged forward into a discordant blend of music and chatter. It was like any public house in Soho on an average Saturday night, crowded with drunks, dense as a smoking battlefield and hosting a central dance floor. Except that everyone inside seemed to be male, of course. And the atmosphere became instantly cooler, as though there were vents somewhere.'

'So it was definitely Pyotr's Cave?' I asked.

'Indeed it was, Watson. A huge bunker, hewn out of raw granite and smoothed over with cement. Large holes ranged around the cavern wall for private trysts. Couples slow-danced to the music and kissed.'

'All right, Holmes. You don't have to go into that much detail.'

'Poor Watson. You just will not accept the fact that some men are sexually attracted to other men. And some women to other women, of course.'

I sat up abruptly.

'What on earth do you mean, Holmes? Musical women?'

'Exactly. The police informed me later on that Virginia Woolf had been caught there, with another of that Bloomsbury lot, Vita Sackville-West, indulging in the cult of Lesbos within one of the caves. Fortunately for them, there's no law against it, unlike with men.'

'Woman with woman? What? How? But there's no ...! Good God almighty!' Now I had heard everything. It simply beggared belief.

'Well. As far as the Bloomsbury Group goes, I imagine that it is not the expression of the feeling that matters, as much as the feeling itself.'

'Stop. That's enough, Holmes. You don't have to elaborate. What happened next?' There are some things that I would never understand.

'Lestrade and I strolled up to the bar and ordered a couple of martinis. We sipped them nonchalantly and pretended to chat while examining the clientele for familiar faces, without any luck. Most of the men were quite ordinary looking people, the type who worked in offices during the day and whom you would pass by on the street without a backward glance. Sadly, they seemed much more interested in my young friend than in the great detective. Joke, Watson. Calm down. Then the music changed back to the dramatic entrance of the Lilac Fairy. There was a sudden hush, the floor cleared and a tiny hairless figure dressed only in a transparent purple tutu danced into the centre, his body glistening with some kind of oil. I nudged Lestrade in excitement. It was my little taxi driver, Ifan Rees. Suddenly many of the unlikely events of the past week began to make a great deal of sense to me. Of course. Rees and Arthur.

That was how they had tracked me. Together they must be the killers.'

'Yes. The filthy little worm was Arthur's grandson. They kidnapped me in Gordon Square.'

'Indeed. He seemed to have inherited his grandfather's mental problems, right enough. The crowd started to laugh and clap as Ifan jumped and twirled like a pink baby hippopotamus around the floor.'

'Oh, dear God. That doesn't bear thinking about,' I interjected.

'It was just good clean fun, Watson. That was when I first recognised my childhood friend, Conan Arthur, the raddled man in that Gordon Square photograph. He had emerged from one of the holes in the wall with a scrawny youth, who looked like one of those rent boys one reads about. You know. A rough type. They hang around Piccadilly Circus quite a lot.'

'Do they? No. I didn't know that, Holmes.' Surprise, surprise. How in blazes *would* I know that?

'He didn't notice me at first. Eventually Rees came to a stand-still beside a microphone to the rear of the bunker, and proceeded to sing a version of the song *Three Little Maids* from *The Mikado* in a high-pitched falsetto:

"One little maid from school am I,
Pert as a school-girl well can be,
Filled to the brim with girlish glee,
One little maid from school!
One little maid who, all unwary,
Comes from a ladies' seminary,
Freed from its genius tutelary

One little maid from school!
One little maid from sch ..."'

'All right, Holmes. In heaven's name, stop! You're singing! Do get on with the story,' I demanded impatiently.

'What's the matter, Watson? Don't you like my voice? You have to imagine a thirty-piece orchestra. Now take it easy. Just another joke. Once the song came to an end and the applause ceased, the hippo bounced his way out of the bunker by another door to the rear. That was when Conan Arthur, fingering his rather twee goatee, stared over at the bar and perceived his childhood nemesis for the first time. The look of astonishment on his face was something to behold, but it was swiftly replaced by one of extreme fear as I raised my stick sword and pointed it at him accusingly, like a rapier in advance of an attack. He handed something to the young boy beside him and started walking – running, really – after Rees through the rear exit. I grabbed Lestrade and pulled him with me across the dance floor and after the murderous pair of serial killers.'

'It was time for the vengeance of Sherlock Holmes.'

Chapter XVII.

The Diogenes Club.

'We chased my so-called childhood friend down a labyrinthine warren of narrow, undulating passages, with Lestrade taking the lead. He had almost caught up with him when we came to another blank wall. And Conan turned on us.

' "If you kill me, I promise that you will never find your Boswell, Sherlock," he snarled, like a cornered rat. "Your oh-so-literary doctor lover will die, starving and all alone. And in great pain." '

'I unsheathed my stick sword, fully prepared to run him through right there and then, regardless of right or wrong. For my father and my brother, Watson. And for the insult to you, of course. But I realised what he was saying, and held back. And that was when we heard these breathless, whispered words behind us:

' "One little maid from school am I,
Pert as a school-girl well can be,
Filled to the brim with girlish glee ..."

We wheeled around to find the appalling sight of a completely naked hippopotamus, Ifan Rees, tutu-less and his skin gleaming in the candlelight. He was tossing his slaughter knife from hand to hand and laughing to himself, as he prepared to attack. Lestrade withdrew his Bulldog and pointed it at the lunatic.'

' "Put down the knife, or I will shoot you," he commanded.'

‘ “One little maid from school!
One little maid who, all unwary,
Comes from a ladies’ semin ...” ’

‘Rees danced forwards, feigning to cut Lestrade’s throat with the knife. The Scotland Yard detective swayed back, and then warned him again.’

‘ “Do you actually *want* to die?” queried Lestrade in alarm.’

‘ “Freed from its genius tutelary
One little maid from school!
One little maid from sch ...” ’

‘Rees lunged at the Scotland Yard detective and Lestrade shot him once through the throat. The cab-driver stopped in his stride, staggered, dropped his knife, grabbed his neck as though he wanted to hold the skin together, spat a gout of thick blood from his throat, smiled enigmatically, and fell to the floor dead as a doornail. Do please forgive the dramatic clichés, Watson.’

‘Oh, don’t worry. I know all about clichés. They can come in really useful at times. My readers are very familiar with them. They wouldn’t read the stories without those platitudes. Pray continue,’ I yawned.

‘Shortly after the gunshot, I heard Conan Arthur stamping on the ground. I thought it was his rage at the loss of Ifan, but actually he was lifting up the wall and disappearing through it, faster than a vole being chased by a stoat. I was after him like goat’s cheese on a tambourine, leaving Lestrade to call for help and to cope with any hysteria produced by his gunshot. Under no circumstances was Conan going to escape my revenge. I hared after him. Well, not exactly hare, Watson, but as fast as I could, anyway. I remember that we went past the original steps from the garage, in the opposite direction to the Cave.'

'You would have been passing underneath the other garage, then,' I suggested amicably.

'Probably. My only thought was to get the worm who had murdered my brother and father. And threatened to kill me, of course. He was gasping for breath, but still ahead of me, when he reached another set of steps, at the end of that right-hand passage. They were very steep and I too was struggling for air, so I had to stop at the bottom and watch him disappear into the gloom. There were no more candles, you see. Eventually I got back enough wind to follow him up the stairs, and just guess where we came out, Watson.'

'Oh, I don't know. The Ritz?'

'Ha, ha! I wish! It was the gap between the Main Room and the Stranger's Room in the Diogenes Club. We should have examined that area more thoroughly the other day. You know, this case has made me feel that I might be losing my touch a bit. Perhaps I'm not as good as I once was, but still good enough, eh, Watson? Good man. Absolutely right. Say nothing. A simple dummy wall pushed open from the stairs, and there I was. The door to the Stranger's Room was wide open and so I followed my childhood enemy into it, closing it firmly behind me. He lay below the bay window and seemed to be in some sort of agony, wheezing loudly as he struggled for a tablet from his pocket. He raised the palm of one hand, as though begging me to wait just a minute before I ran him through.'

' "Hello, Goatslayer," I muttered, unsheathing my sword. "Long time, no see." '

'He swallowed his pill and stood up shakily, all the while keeping his outstretched hand between us. I waited patiently. There were questions that needed answering. But it was he who asked the first one.'

' "How ... how did you know where we were? I told that poor Welsh idiot to devise some clue that would provide only your name." '

' "His clue was quite simple, Conan. Maybe he wanted to accelerate your plan: *See you, Holmes, at Pyotr's Cave tonight.* Finding the club required a spot of lateral thinking, but we got there eventually. Now. Where is Watson? If you tell me that, I'll make your end blissfully swift. Unlike those you provided for my brother and father." '

' "That was Ifan's doing. He heard voices which told him what to do. The poor lad was mentally ill from early childhood, a schizophrenic they call it nowadays, and would have spent his life behind locked doors if I hadn't offered to look after him. I suspect that he really wanted to cut off his own genitals, but hadn't the courage. And I'm dying anyway. It doesn't really matter how I go to my reward. Oh, Sherlock, don't you remember anything at all about our childhood friendship, our mutual love?" he pleaded.'

' "Not much," I replied. "Apart from a few games we used to play. Anything else is some perverted fantasy your diseased mind has created to keep the flames of your hatred burning. Back then, you became ill in the woods and I had to go and get help for you. There was nothing more to it than that. Now, prepare to meet your Maker." '

'I was about to avenge my family deaths with Conan Arthur when he summoned reserves of strength that I did not expect. Grabbing one of the step-ladders, he flung it through the centre of the bay window, smashing the ventilation fan and the surrounding fruits and family crests and creating a hole large enough for him to crawl through.'

' "Look at me, Sherlock! Love you!" the madman cried, blowing me a kiss as he leapt through the window, thereby depriving me of my just retribution. I ran to the hole and gazed down, to witness his final death throes, surrounded by a pool of his tainted blood that spread slowly around his body and into the gutter of Pall Mall.'

'So there you have it, Watson. He kept up that fantasy of a teenage relationship with me throughout his life, and blamed me and my family for all his subsequent problems. Unfortunately we still had no idea where you might be, until one of Lestrade's constables heard a loud drone coming from within the other garage. It sounded like a malfunctioning motor engine, he said. Starting and stopping. I recognised it! That was when we found you hanging around, fast asleep as usual and snoring your head off. We untied your limbs and granted you the freedom to tell us your version of events and to hear our end of the story, as related by this ancient roué. Let us hope that all musical men in London will sleep safely in their beds from now on. Which reminds me. Why don't you pop off, while I play you a short lullaby?'

Holmes picked up his violin from the mantel, placed it under his chin and started plucking it, *pizzicato* style.

‘Good night, Holmes. Just make it *soave*, will you? Smooth and gentle.’

I shuffled painfully towards the stairs to my old room.

‘Of course, old fellow. Sleep well.’

Epilogue.

And so it was that when Holmes invited me to continue my stay at 221B Baker Street and see out my remaining days in his eccentric company as a twice-widowed bachelor, with no hint whatsoever of the love that dare not speak its name, I accepted with alacrity. After all, we were two halves of the same person, I believe. Like David and Jonathan. One soul in two bodies. I still didn't know the full truth of his teenage behaviour with Conan Arthur, whose story was never corroborated by Holmes himself. And I couldn't love him in the same way that Arthur had loved him. But I loved him yet. Who is to say that Platonic love is less intense or profound than sexual love? I could only hope that my influence might curb his new-found enthusiasm for taking the law into his own hands when pursuing criminals.

I would transfer my small practice back into my old room, and we would continue our detecting while I treated my occasional patients, the pair of us to be kept in line by the wonderful ring mistress Lily, our fellow bloodhound and code-breaker, with young Lestrade to help us out when necessary. I had to reluctantly accept the inevitable passing of time and cease fantasising about our well-endowed housekeeper. There was a chance I might yet be called upon to give her away in holy matrimony to young Jasper one day, and that was definitely worth looking forward to.

It's called retirement by some, but then neither of us anticipated the sheer variety of dark and desperate adventures that lay ahead over the following six years, each of which I have documented separately. Maybe I'll call them '*The Final Tales Of Sherlock Holmes*' and dedicate the collection to the memory of the world's first consulting detective and the straightest friend that any man could have.

You never know.

Some day in the distant future the general public might be ready to appreciate these arcane stories.

WATCH OUT FOR:

1. *Sherlock Holmes And The Hampstead Ponies.*
2. *Sherlock Holmes And The Chelsea Necrophile.*
3. *Sherlock Holmes And The Holland Park Cannibal.*
4. *Sherlock Holmes And The Richmond Werewolf.*
5. *Sherlock Holmes And The Hammersmith Hound.*
6. *Sherlock Holmes And The Shepherds Bushman.*
7. *Sherlock Holmes And The Acton Body-Snatchers.*
8. *Sherlock Holmes And The Notting Hill Rapist.*
9. *Sherlock Holmes And The Clapham Witch.*
10. *Sherlock Holmes And The Battersea Fetishists.*
11. *Sherlock Holmes And The Kew Gardens Gnomes.*
12. *Sherlock Holmes And The Portobello Pornographer.*
13. *Sherlock Holmes And The Camden Counterfeiter.*
14. *Sherlock Holmes And The Kensington Kidnapper.*
15. *Sherlock Holmes And The Undiscovered Country.*

Also From MX Publishing

MX Publishing is the world's largest specialist Sherlock Holmes publisher, with over a hundred titles and fifty authors creating the latest in Sherlock Holmes fiction and non-fiction.

From traditional short stories and novels to travel guides and quiz books, MX Publishing cater for all Holmes fans.

The collection includes leading titles such as *Benedict Cumberbatch In Transition* and *The Norwood Author* which won the 2011 Howlett Award (Sherlock Holmes Book of the Year).

MX Publishing also has one of the largest communities of Holmes fans on Facebook with regular contributions from dozens of authors.

www.mxpublishing.com

Also from MX Publishing

Our bestselling books are our short story collections – of which we have several;

'Lost Stories of Sherlock Holmes' , 'The Outstanding Mysteries of Sherlock Holmes', The Papers of Sherlock Holmes Volume 1 and 2, 'Untold Adventures of Sherlock Holmes' (and the sequel 'Studies in Legacy) and 'Sherlock Holmes in Pursuit', 'The Cotswold Werewolf and Other Stories of Sherlock Holmes' – and many more……

www.mxpublishing.com

Links

MX Publishing are proud to support the Save Undershaw campaign – the campaign to save and restore Sir Arthur Conan Doyle's former home. Undershaw is where he brought Sherlock Holmes back to life, and should be preserved for future generations of Holmes fans.

SaveUndershaw
www.saveundershaw.com

Sherlockology
www.sherlockology.com

MX Publishing
www.mxpublishing.com

You can read more about Sir Arthur Conan Doyle and Undershaw in Alistair Duncan's book (share of royalties to the Undershaw Preservation Trust) – *An Entirely New Country* and in the amazing compilation *Sherlock's Home – The Empty House* (all royalties to the Trust).

www.ingramcontent.com/pod-product-compliance
Lightning Source LLC
LaVergne TN
LVHW012331100826
845148LV00017B/2106
* 9 7 8 1 7 8 0 9 2 5 6 5 3 *